Sound

By Kelly Bruno

This book is a work of fiction. The characters, incidents, and dialogues are products of the author's imagination and are not to be construed as real. Any resemblance to actual persons, living or dead, is entirely coincidental.

FIRST EDITION PUBLISHED 2014

SECOND EDITION 2016

Cover art and print/ebook design

by East Coast Designs

www.eastcoastdesigns.ca

ISBN 978-1-7772632-4-9

Imperceptions

Imperceptions Press
Oromocto, New Brunswick
www.imperceptions-press.com

Please note that this book was edited on a donation basis for Misophonia International. For any errors, we apologize as this was done as a work of advocacy.

This book is dedicated to all who seek
the answers and to all who
continue to fight forward in our battle for
Misophonia research and awareness.

The sounds. They're slowly transforming one by one. Pounding. Drumming. Never dwindling away down a paraded street. Taking no interest in my heart. Only my brain. Only my thoughts. My thoughts. Constantly snapped, clicked, banged out of existence. My brain. Alone. Beating. Destructing. Diminishing. Creating. The rage. There is no escape

August 2011

Summer is coming to an end once again. The nights are getting cooler and our front tree's top is becoming ominously orange. Soon, all around us, will be the colors of poisonous snakes and frogs from afar, hissing down from above. People will come from miles around to observe the sure death of all that's green and warm. We're off, heading to the mall for school shopping. I'm stuck in the backseat with Gum Smacker. Why can't he chew with his mouth shut? My whole body is cringing from his smack, smack, smack. I'd like to just smack, smack, smack his face. I open the window all the way down, turning my face just right so the incoming wind can tornado deep down into my right ear. I stuff my finger as far as imaginable into my left ear, teasing my eardrum with never mending damage. But I don't care.

Maybe my life would be better if I couldn't hear at all. Every smack of Gum Smacker's gum jeers a tingling pain up into my head. The tingling is nothing new, though. I first noticed it in the second grade.

I'm stuck next to Emma in class. She's ok. That is, ok from a distance. All the other girls like her. But me, I have to sit next to her. All day. And all day long her tongue becomes a suction cup, suctioning up onto her mouth rooftop and snapping down. A wet, suction-snap. I might as well walk up to the chalkboard and—well, you know what—with my fingernails. All day long. Over and over again. It wouldn't bother me. But then, well, at least maybe then she would know how it feels.

*

We're finally at the mall and Mom is telling me I'd better fix my hair. The noise muffling wind has taken its toll. I quickly grab my brush from my purse and swipe my brown frizzy locks down over my ears, my last defense against Gum Smacker. Abby is already here waiting for me. Mom lets us go on our separate way; we'll meet at the food court in an hour. She and Dad will help Jeffery with his Kindergarten shopping while Abby and I head out for fashion!

"What happened to you?" she laughs, obviously observing my whirlwind hairdo.

"Brother love," is all I have to say. We head into the first store and Abby is already eyeing the jeans rack.

"Too long…too blue…too..." she mumbles under her breath, fingering through the selections. This is why she's my best friend. No one

is more intensely picky than she is, than I

am. She doesn't think so, though. She says I have no fashion sense. I search and search through the same racks as she does. She knows the new season's style before the runway models can stretch their long legs down the aisle. She's now holding up a size 1 to her toddler sized waist. I know what's next as her slanted hazel eyes size me up and down. Her teeth are beaming out her satisfaction as she lifts off the rack an identical jean, just, well, a few sizes bigger. She doesn't even have to ask my size.

"Come on!" She grabs my wrist and takes the lead to the dressing rooms.

In my dressing room the smile shudders off my lips. I look inside the jeans and meet my dread. It's all there—the long scratchy seams stemming from the bottom of the ankles all the way up to the waist. Why not just line the jeans with cactus? And then there's the tag that will never cut off no matter how close I could ever possibly cut it. Even if I could, it would leave little prickly strings in its place. I would surely cut and pick until there was nothing left but a hole. Would anyone notice the draft in the back of my seat?

I undress and stare into the legs of the jeans once more. Maybe I can wear leggings under them. I wish I had some leggings right now. My head prickles. I scrunch one foot carefully into the opening. The seam is already rubbing the side of my foot; cactus needles spray up my leg and into my spine. I have to move faster. I yank the jeans up my leg, gasping in a breath, but I can't breathe back out. My body convulses. I force my breath out. Now the other leg. It's no easier, but I jerk them up quickly. My body has become the body of the cactus.

Stiff, prickly, fierce. I've gotten the jeans around my waist, but I can't button them—not yet. My fingers grasp the back of my underpants and yank them up protecting my unexpectant, exposed skin from the shock of the tag. Finally, they're on. I look in the mirror. My face is pale, but the jeans are perfect. Why do they have to be perfect?

Dr. Angle once told Mom that I have tactile dysfunction. Or, in Mom's words, sensory issues. Me, I just say it how it is: I was the infant who they thought was colicky; I cried for hours, never giving in (not until winter ended and summer began, when it was too hot for my once-too-many-times-washed, scratchy polyester PJs). I was the toddler, bursting through the yard, leaving a trail of clothing behind me, shrieking, and laughing, my naked butt shining in broad daylight for all to see. I was the preschooler, sprawled across the classroom floor in a full-fledged kicking and thrashing tantrum, refusing to put back on my bunchy, toe seamed socks over my air-gasping feet.

And I was, and still am, the girl who will only wear cotton clothing, with minimum seams touching my body, who wears certain clothes inside-out, who cringes at even the thought of the wrong material touching my skin.

Abby peeks in on me now with her glowing cheeks. She whips the curtain open and poses her runway pose in her identical cactus torture.

"Love 'em!" her voice gleams. "We have to have them!" I manage to smile back. She is my new shopping mom, picking out clothes that I secretly loathe, and then there's me, faking a smile and pretending to agree.

Mom, Dad, and Jeffery are already waiting at the food court as we arrive. Dad's checking his watch. I know his irritated frown all too well. And worse, his sickening teeth sucking habit that goes along with it. Ever since I can remember he's had this habit, a memory I wish I could forget.

The kitchen tiles, new, opal swirled, glazed with wax under bare muddy feet. I leap, intentionally, square to square. My prints, perfect—symmetrically placed. So I think. But not him. A sound is coming out from within his tightly pinched lips. Lips that are thin. Lips that are curling unnaturally down. A noise that offends my ears, even though it is not a word. Air where there is no air. Only teeth. Only tongue. Open your mouth. Let in the air. No. Only the noise. His eyes are burning into my art upon the floor. I want him to yell. I want him to whip his hand across my butt. Breathe! Open your mouth! He does. I do not care what he says. I am better now. The sound is gone.

*

My feet start to slag in anticipation. A sharp pain is jabbing at my right temple. Abby stops to look back at me.

"Come on, Jess! Your dad looks pissed!" I try to walk faster.

My feet make it, but I can't make out his words. All I hear is tongue on teeth. Anger. Tongue. Knives piercing my skull. Is the anger his or mine? I can't comprehend my own mind.

"Sorry Dad. We lost track of time." My voice doesn't match my emotion. My eyes drift to the ground, far away from the grimacing sound of his mouth. How can anyone look at him? Now Jeffrey's at my feet laughing, poking my side with his finger. "You're in trouble! You're in trouble!"

Abby's slanted eyes are no longer slanted. I never knew they could grow so round.

"Jeffery, that's enough."

Mom grabs his hand pulling his chanting body away from me.

"Do you have another headache, Jess?"

My eyes won't meet hers, only the floor.

"Yeah." If that's what you want to call it.

I don't know if Dad is still sucking his teeth, but the noise is engraved in my brain, grinding my temple, sucking my lifespan out through my ear canals. I need to plug them shut. Now.

"I'll make you an appointment with Dr. Angle," Mom decides. I don't respond. She doesn't understand. How could she?

September

Sitting up on the examination table, I drudgingly study Mom's long-ago-youthful hair. Her wavy brown hair now droops down, just lapping the tips of her shoulder blades like a beagle's soft ears. In pictures, before I was born, her hair was alive. It swooshed down the middle of her back like the waves of the ocean, tinted golden, reflecting the sun. Now it only reflects the florescent light of the doctor's office, awkwardly, revealing silver-sparkling highlights, shining out her age. I will dye mine.

Mom looks up at me.

"Hmm, he should be here real soon," she tries to reassure me.

I'd rather not be reassured. I'd rather sit here all day dully studying her graying hair than face a doctor that I will knowingly lie to. It's not that I want to lie. It's really that he won't believe the truth. The truth that with every little click, every little smack my brother makes with his mouth, and every single time my father's tongue angrily sucks his teeth—noises so indescribably irritating—my temple's fragile, fuzzy tingling turns into a raging pot of self-inflicting pain. No, I will only tell him that I have headaches. And, he will tell Mom to give me Tylenol. The end.

My life is never so easy. Once he walks in, Mom openly indulges in her own opinion. "Dr. Angle," she says, "I know that these headaches are not normal. Jessica has them almost on a daily basis. And—I'm sorry Jessica—but her attitude is really changing…for the worse."

Sorry, Jessica? Really? My mouth won't open to release the words. "How would you describe her attitude changing?" Dr. Angle readies his pen above his clipboard, looking at Mom, not me. I suppose he'll write this new information down, too.

"Well, she is really…well, miserable." Side glance at me, "She locks herself in her bedroom. She won't talk to her brother, and she refuses to even eat dinner with us anymore." Her eyebrows raise up and down, teasing crinkly lines on her forehead that form, disappear, form. Her forehead doesn't give in to her eyebrows' taunt, however. Her eyebrows' stubbly hairs will never reach the fine lines that come and go with persuasion, but her left eye twitches its discomfort.

Dr. Angle writes it all down. He looks at Mom, as I seem to have disappeared from the room.

"How long would you say this has been going on?" She looks at him uncertainly.

"Um, well, I'm not so sure. A good few months, I'd say." A pause. Mom looks at him again. I guess I'm still not here? "No, probably more," she continues. And continues…

I am the child stuck on the swing, clenching its chains. Mom and Dr. Angle think I don't know how to pump my feet. They are the two big kids rushing me back and forth. One in front, one behind. Her way, his way, her way, his. Their ideas don't match my own on how this ride is supposed to turn out. Mine: close to the ground, safe.

Theirs: abrupt, high, angular, the ground swooping in and out of sight. I feel sick. No Tylenol. They call in for the grown-ups, who will do the pushing from now on. A neurologist and a therapist. This is not how the ride was supposed to turn out.

Mom's already on me as soon as we get home. She says that I have to eat at the dinner table tonight, "just like everyone else." I knew this was coming. She listens to everything that Dr. Angle tells her. He went on and on about the values of families dining together: the long conversations of how everyone's day went, the 'sacredness' of just being together in silence. He does not know our family. He does not know about the open-while-stuffed-mouth, smacking and belching, disgusting little brother who sits directly across from his sister. He does not know about the un-sacred, silent glares that ream out of the sister's eyes, burning deathly holes into the source of the obnoxiousness. He does not hear the sucking of teeth of the father who catches the flash of flames darting across the table, from the corner of his eye. There are no values here.

*

But anyway, here I sit. Spaghetti and meatball night. One minute in and my temple has already begun to crawl within itself. A spider's fat back, bubbling, deep inside my pulsing vein. Its legs creeping under-neath the layers of my skin. Venom escaping, seeping up into my brain as I watch long, sauce smothered spaghetti swirl around and around his fork. His mouth opens wide with anticipation. His tongue, moist, ready to devour; devour me insane, for his lips will not shut again.

They do not shut again…

Smack. The sound is here, caught in the spider's web. Snagged.

Snarling around and around and around my vein. Tighter and tighter. I feel the pain, the buildup. The restricted rage… Smack. His tongue suctions his spaghetti stuffed mouth once again…

Smash! Venom erupts. My plate has exploded across the room in a fly's helpless rage. I'm standing. Dad is standing. Tongue sucks teeth. I hear screaming.

"Shut up! All of you! Stop making that sound!"

It was me. Tears are flooding my cheeks. Feet are fleeing me out the door, running me down the street. Running…What just happened?

The rage is still rushing through my veins as I make my escape through the darkened neighborhood streets. I hear Mom's voice calling me back, but I will not stop. Her voice is slowly being crumpled up by the crunching of browning leaves and the twigs of maple and elm underneath my feet. And I am glad. I need to get away. It was her fault. She made me sit there. She made me sit there and listen to his obnoxious sounds. He does it on purpose—I know he does. Just to bother me. Every time we sit down to eat dinner, he smiles his disgusting smile and then just starts smacking with his mouth wide open.

Why doesn't she teach him some manners? He's so gross. I hate him. I hate him!

Going back home is not easy. Someone will be there waiting for me.

Waiting to talk. But my voice will not be heard. I walk slowly up my front steps, fixating my night strained eyes onto their smooth marble surface that captures the moon's obscure glow. I sit down. My fingers move slowly across the stone. Back and forth, they feel the past. They long for what was, for Grandpa. He built the steps when I was just a baby. Mom says I used to sit in the grass, picking through the dirt and the bugs that dared to come near me, and watch Grandpa in awe. I wish I could remember. I do remember him, though. His strong arms with puffy blue-green veins and drooping wrinkly skin. The brown of his eyes, so dark that the little black dots in the centers played hide- and-seek with my eyes that looked back into his. His eyebrows, curly thick, white like cotton, playfully curving over his eyes. His smile, small underneath his heavy mustache, but always true. If he were here, he would hear me. He would listen to my words, even if there were none. He would know that I am sorry, that I miss eating dinner with my family. If only they didn't have to make those sounds.

What waits for me instead is not Grandpa. Actually, it isn't anyone. The house is silent. Jeffery is tucked in his bed. Mom is reading on the couch. Dad is smoking out on the back deck. Do they even remember that I was gone? I slip away into my bedroom, seemingly unnoticed. And then, there it is. Not a someone, but rather a something, waiting for me, lifeless on my rumpled bed. A single folded up piece of paper. A simple note that, I'm certain, possesses my future. I'm not sure that I want to unfold it. But I do:

Jessica,

We called the crisis center while you were gone. We have an appointment tomorrow morning at ten. We will talk then.

Mom and Dad

Crisis Center? Why there? They are the crisis. They will never understand.

All the way to the crisis center, no one talks. Jeffery is with us, too, but he doesn't look at me. No one looks at anyone. Mom scheduled the appointment for the whole family. I secretly hope that the councilor will lock Jeffery up after hearing just the slightest mouth smack escape from his lips. Or better yet, go ahead and lock me up. The psychiatric patients there probably have better manners than any single person in my whole family. But of course, neither happens.

Ms. Shay leads us to her office, pulling in an extra chair from the hallway behind her. She delicately holds out her hand, guiding my parents to the love seat. She then sweeps her hand to the right, persuading my body to the oversized and stuffed lavender recliner. Jeffery will have the cushioned folding chair from the hall, to the left of Mom and Dad. Ms. Shay's fingers pat it gently, and Jeffery's body obeys her silent command. Her own chair allows her to roll and swivel in any direction that she pleases. She glides into the opening between Jeffery and me. She has placed us carefully into a perfect circle. Every movement she makes is swift and graceful. Her voice is soft. I almost like her. That is, until the questions begin.

She ruffles through the paperwork Mom had filled out in the waiting room and asks us all some basic questions: our ages, where we go to school, Mom and Dad's jobs, how many bedrooms we have, what our social lives are like, blah, blah, blah. I can tell that her main point is to find out more about me as she rarely looks away from me. Mom does most of the talking, but no one seems to look away from me. I might as well have been placed in the center of the ring like a tacky dining table centerpiece, so all eyes could gawk at me disapprovingly. They do anyway.

"So, Jessica, would you like to begin our discussion with your feelings about last night?" She finally asks the question. Her big brown cow eyes try to milk mine for a response.

I look away. I'm done talking for the day. Why doesn't she just ask Mom? Mom seems to have all the answers. I surely didn't call for this meeting.

No one speaks. I stare at the cheap,

checkered, wearing rug. I feel the gawking. I carefully finger comb and stretch down my tight locks, my personal gate, blocking the brown cows from entering my green pastures.

Silence.

Locked out, the cows turn to new fields for grazing.

"Dianne, last night when we talked on the phone, you sounded concerned for Jessica's well-being. Would you like to begin our discussion with any thoughts that you may be feeling now?"

This time Mom doesn't have a chance. Dad intercepts.

"We've had it with her. I mean, look at her! Even now she's hiding under her hair. She never talks, she just storms around the house talking to no one, slamming doors, and...and last night was the last straw!"

"Hmm." Pause. "Jessica, would you like to try to talk to your parents now, here with me?"

Silence.

Jeffery flops in his seat. "Jess?" Mom tries.

SOUND

Silence.

Dad: "She won't talk to any of you! Maybe if you push her long enough she'll smash a window and scream for all of us to shut up!"

Tongue sucks teeth. Jab in temple.

Silence.

"Maybe it would be helpful for Jessica to talk with me in private first. That is, if it is ok with you, Dianne and Greg? You can wait in the lobby with Jeffery and we will call you back in, in say, about ten minutes?"

Dad reluctantly follows Mom out the door. A mix of Dad's muffled ranting and Jeffery's shrill imaginary superhero impressions trail down the hallway, farther and farther away.

Cows invade pastures.

The questions that come next were not what I had expected. Their focus suddenly turns toward my family: Does anyone harm me? Do I ever feel unsafe? Am I abused in anyway?

Is she for real? The only abuse comes from

what's inside of me. How do I explain that? I hear my voice answering her.

"No...No...No." I don't.

She asks again about last night. My voice turns silent. This meeting is pointless.

She reminds me that anything I tell her is completely confidential: she is not allowed to repeat anything to my parents. I'm not sure what the answers are that she is looking for. I do know that I do not have them. She may be the therapist, but I can easily detect her secret frustration with me. She finds nothing. She will only find nothing. I want to leave.

Mom, Dad and Jeffery are called back in. We are soon on our way out the door.

"Well, at least she was able to refer you to a good counselor, Jess.

It's actually one of the ones that Dr. Angle had suggested." Mom's face twists back to look at me. Her smile seems as crooked as her twisted neck.

My stare turns blankly away, out the window. I can't get home soon enough.

October

Thin, jagged twigs intertwine. Eyes follow their inward passage: light to dark, thin to thick, deeper inward, moving unprotected, swallowed inside the unexplored gapping crevices of the young tree's trunk. Alone. My eyes close. We are one. Alone…

"Jess!" Abby's alarmed yelp awakens me. My eyes open to find hazel ovals inquisitively inspecting me over. "What are you doing out here?" Trepidation has overcome her voice. Her hands grasp mine and heave my now roused body to an upward sitting position. She is squatting down. We're eye to eye, "You have to come back. Everyone's looking for you. What happened?"

*

Biology class is second period every day. I'm here once again, forced into the clicking madness. A new sound; an old reaction. Every day. Today, Paul sits be- hind me, fidgeting, clicking his pen. Mrs. Adams paces in front of me, click, click, clicking back and forth. I am surrounded. The ears all around me are oblivious; the sounds enter in and current out; an undetected ripple flowing down a stream. Only I am stuck in that ripple. Drowning—a tiny ant trapped and tortured.

Pens and heels click, click, clicking me down under the water. Whirlpools twist forcefully through unprotected ear canals, raging waters flooding my brain. Water pushing, pushing behind my eyes' dams, threatening to overflow and pour out, down over the open fields of flushing cheeks for all to see. I would rather drown internally. But the clicking spasms are too strong; they are forcing the water through the dams. Down over the fields. All can see. Do they see? I have to escape. The sounds. The eyes. They're all over me.

I, a tiny ant, escape the flood. Out into the open I run. Outdoors, across the field to a tree. I collapse down, facing the tree, and then fall onto my back, staring up. Staring. Taking it in. Letting it go...

*

Now Abby has found me.

"Who's 'everyone'?" I answer finally.

Abby picks dead leaves out of my tangled locks. "Who do you think?" her voice is impatient. She hastily brushes more leaves off of my back and shoulders, "Get up! By now they've called your mother for sure."

She quickly leads the way back across the football field and through the school doors. Mr. Owens, the vice-principal, is already there, waiting. I hear Abby's mouth utter a startled gasp.

"Abby, get back to class," his voice is a raspy death. "Jessica, you're with me. Now."

Simultaneously we obey and head off on our separate ways. There is no escaping this.

Mom is already in Mr. Owens' office when I arrive. Was I really gone that long? I don't know. What I do know is that this is not going to be good. And for sure, listening to Mr. Owens' lecture is really not going to be good.

Every morning, at precisely 7:22 am, my ears are 'welcomed' into the school by Mr. Owens' loudspeaker greeting. Every morning my temple crumbles within itself, gritting with pain, with the first click of the loudspeaker turning on, knowing his voice will follow. My fingers dig deep, desperately, trying to plug up my ears. It never works. Every day I am condemned to start the day off on the wrong note.

Now the anguish coming up from Mr. Owens' tar-infested lungs coarsely invades my brain as he wheezes and hacks out his lengthy lecture of why it is not only "unacceptable" to walk out of a classroom, but school grounds. Technically, I never left the school grounds, but

SOUND

I haven't the slightest desire to fight my case. That would only lengthen the time my ears will have to endure the scouring sounds of Mr.

Owens' sandpaper voice. I'm not sure of half of what he is saying to me. I only know that he is angry. And I, too, am becoming enraged. Each word that grates through his teeth, each mucus stuffed hack that never quite frees his crisped lungs and throat from smoker's phlegm is sanding my ears, my temple, and my brain into a very fine point.

A point that I imagine myself thrusting straight through his antagonizing throat. Clearing him a new passageway. A new clean hole in which to breath from. Speak from. One that is quiet.

My eyes squeeze shut. My fingers are digging deep into my ears. My head is down on Mr. Owens' desk. I need to escape...

"Jessica?" Her voice emerges through my finger plugs, a memory of talking deep under water.

"Jessica?" Her hand is on my shoulder.

Mom's newfound warmth lifts my head to shore.

I look up. Water pours down over my face. Again.

Upon the inspection of my soaked cheeks, Mom's forehead crinkles.

Deep lines push her eyebrows down into sullen frowns. But her eyes rebel against her anger, bright and moist, they speak her concern and her fear.

I take my finger out of one ear and clench the hair above my right temple. My left finger stays defensively in place. The torture is not yet through.

"Why did you run out of class?" Mom's voice is a strange, yet brings a short-lived wave of relief. I know that the wave will be dragged back out into the sea just as quickly as it has come in.

And anyway, I have no answer. My sanded brain's thoughts are blowing around in its own dust. Mr. Owens' ear-grinded dust. What could I possibly say? Mrs. Adams' heels click when she walks? Paul keeps clicking his pen? My eyes close. Tight. I try to envision the tree. I can only envision Mr. Owens' mouth forcing out his wheezing, gritty words. I long for the tree's peace. Its silence. But the sand is clouding my brain. A storm of dust is taking form. Swirling madness inside my head.

"If there is a problem in Mrs. Adams' class, now is the time to talk about it."

His sentence is too long, his words too raspy, the pain too intense.

The dust. A full blown sandstorm. Raging. I feel my eyes growing wide. Burning. There's hair ripping out, tangling around the fingers of my right hand. My body is rising and it will not go back down. Deathly sounds are telling me to sit back down. I will not. I can't see the way out but I know it is there.

I'm sitting in a familiar room. I'm listening to an unfamiliar story. It is supposed to be my story. The story about my day. About me, today. But it is not my story, for I am not the one telling it. It is being told by someone else. Someone else who has gathered the facts. Facts that were gathered by looking from the outside in. Not from the inside out.

Mom is the storyteller. She is telling Ms. Shay her story, her story about me. A story that is not true. Is it?

Really, I'm not sure what my story is. Maybe I am crazy. Maybe I do belong here, at the Crisis Center. I mean, how can a sound, a little click, send me storming out of class? How can the sound of some- one's voice force my own fingers to rip clumps of my own hair out of my own head? How can these little, everyday sounds, drown my face with my own tears? I really am crazy. I must be.

But, no. If I am crazy, then why do I feel pain? Pain that is real, pain that comes from within my raging head. The dagger that splits open my right temple, grinding and twisting with every offending sound.

Maybe I'm not crazy. Maybe something is very wrong inside my head. Inside my brain.

Growing. A tumor. Somewhere between my ears and my brain.

"Mom!" The eruption of my voice breaks apart their conversation.

Four eyes widen and stare back into mine.

"It's my head. The sounds. I can't stand the sound." Tears are forming behind my eyes. I cannot let them fall. Not this time.

"What sounds, Jessica?"

"Clicking. All the clicking. It won't stop. My head is going to explode." I said too much. The tears are making their escape. Their familiar flight, straight down my face. I know by the looks on their faces that I should have kept my mouth shut. Why did I not keep my mouth shut?

"Clicking?" Mom's voice quivers.

"What kind of clicking do you hear, Jessica?" Ms. Shay's pen is ready.

What kind of clicking? There are different kinds of clicking?

"J...just clicking." Great! What kind of an

answer was that?

"I mean, when I hear clicking sounds it makes my head…hurt." My head is starting to hurt right now. Someone please, shut me up!

"Jess, your appointment with the neurologist is not until the beginning of next month."

"She has an appointment with a neurologist?"

"Yes, we scheduled it back in September. She has been having headaches for a while now."

Mom's eyebrows take a sudden crash dive down. Crumpling down, frowning at her newfound ignorance. Her eyes flare into mine.

"Why didn't you tell me about the sounds, Jessica?" Her cheeks flush.

"I…I don't know." I wonder too… Why not? Because she would think that I am crazy, that's why. But would she think I'm crazy? Does she? I don't know.

"How often do you hear these sounds, Jessica?" Ms. Shay's lips are forming a smile. A smile that is supposed to sooth a baby. A smile that is supposed to say, "It's ok, you can trust me." A smile that is sup- posed to lead you into saying things that you would normally not tell anyone, not even your best friend. I know her smile. I do not like her smile. I do not like her.

I don't answer.

Finally, my mouth is shut. "Jess?"

"Jessica, it's ok to tell us what is bothering you. We are here to help you. I know that I may not have all of the answers, but I will do my best to try and help figure things out." Quick breath. "If we work together, maybe I can help you."

Her pen waits in silence.

Her soothing smile fades away.

Stubbly eyebrows rise slowly to the snow tinted mountaintop. I look away.

I study the familiar, worn, cheap checkered rug. Why did I open my mouth?

*

Home at last. Unfortunately, I still cannot relax. Mom and Ms. Shay made me an appointment with Lisa, the therapist to whom Mom was supposed to send me back in September. The therapist who both Ms. Shay and Dr. Angle had suggested. Ms. Shay told Mom that it seems

I am having anxiety attacks, and not only that, but she feels it would be "wise for Jessica to go through a psychological evaluation." How do they plan on evaluating me? Hook me up with clicking sounds in hopes to rage my brain? "Yes," they'd say, "she is crazy."

Right now, I just need to lay down and fall asleep. Pretend to sleep. Anything. Before the day gets any worse. Before Dad gets home. With his sound. His tongue, teeth, lips, squeezing out that sound…

Morning took forever to get here, but it has finally arrived. I watch it as it rises through the horizontal cracks in my bedroom blinds. The sun, yellow and bright. Contrasting the dark horizontal lines that cross my sight when I tried to look away. Dark. Dark as the night that I didn't sleep through. Dark as the day that surely awaits me. I'll spend it alone. Alone, with in-house suspension for yesterday's tearing out of school doors. Well, almost alone. Today's darkest hours will be shared with an irritable, underpaid substitute teacher. They'll be shared with another kid like me, who tried to escape school but failed. I just hope that neither of them tries to click, click, click their dark, weary torture of a day away with the tip of a pen or the sole of a shoe. Or worse, with a wet, wide-open, gum chewing, smacking mouth, drawing their dark torture into mine. Reawakening my rage, a rage that I can no longer control. One that I can no longer contain inside the darkening depths of my undiagnosed, crazed and raging brain.

Rage without a name...

*

Sleep has found me. It has found me along with something else. Or rather, someone else. Someone's foot is nudging mine underneath my makeshift wood-and-metal bed, my desk. I peek out above my drooly arm, knowing my forehead must have a nice, perfectly round red mark where it has spent the last hour asleep. I discretely rub my sleep-moist chin on a dry part of my sleeve and quickly pull my locks down over my bull's eye forehead. Luckily, he's not looking at me. His silk black hair only halfway hides his squinting brown eyes and freckled nose.

Squinting eyes that are watching the reading eyes of the teacher. She never looks away from her book. His hand slides me a note under- neath my desk. His lips smile as his hand feels mine take the note away from his.

I read his note and feel the heat rising up from my chest, into my cheeks. If he reached over to me now with a marshmallow on a stick it would surely roast to perfection. I'm not sure if my inner bomb-fire was ignited by the instant embarrassment or just the pure, sudden irritation. How did he, Brandon, hear about my day yesterday? I know now that my story must have been the highlight of Blab Central all throughout the school. I can feel Brandon's brown eyes sneaking out from underneath his silky black disguise, watching my every expression. He wants to know why I ran out of Mrs. Adams' class. I will not tell him. His note is crumpling within my fiery fist. I drop it on the floor. Two green lasers aim and burn the squinty brown eyes that once

smiled. My bull's eye forehead resumes its position on my desk. I wish for sleep. No, I wish for death. My life couldn't get any worse. First my inner sanity, now my outer. It is all gone. It's all gone, and now every- one can see it's gone.

With my head on my desk I feel the thoughts overcrowding, squeezing down, suffocating my brain. Jeffery, Dad, Paul, Mrs. Adams, Mr. Owens, the tingling, the sounds. The sounds. Nothing makes sense. Yesterday...last month. No, every day. Today. It used to be only once in a while. It used to be only Jeffery. No, Jeffery and Dad. Dad came first. But what about Emma in second grade? It was her, too.

And were there others?

But why him? Why my own dad? Wasn't there a time when his sounds didn't bother me? A time when we were happy? Sometimes small images float through my head, mix into my dreams. I want them to be real. They have to be…

Strong, furry arms are lifting me up high. High up into the clouds. Beyond the sky. Outer space! Then down, down, down torpedoes my body. My stomach is left behind, up in the stars. It finds its way back to me just as my ears hear my throat's own delighted squeal. My body soars to the ground, skimming the itchy, tall grass, then back up, up, back into the sky. This time I fly free. Free above curly brown hair. Free away from the rough, thick fingers and furry arms that protect me. My lungs shriek their elated shock. He catches me. My ears mix with his deep laughter and the small voice of my own. Strong, furry arms hug me.

Little feet touch the ground. Rough, thick fingers hold my hand. Our arms swing in rhythm to the movement of our bodies, together, hands connected as we walk side by side. Me and my dad.

*

I don't know exactly when the sounds began to secretly steal away my life. My sanity. When they abducted the pathway from my ear- drums on up to my brain. When the fumes of rage leaked into that pathway. But they did. And now they are inviting their friends. More sounds with which to invade my brain. A house party of rage. No one was invited by me, but they are here. And not only are they here, but they are everywhere. Everywhere I go they are there. Small sounds that have always existed. Small sounds that enter into my eardrums every day. The same sounds that I heard as a baby, as a small child, that I heard just a year ago. They have changed. One by one, when they enter in through my eardrums and move on up to my brain, they have decided that they will take a new course. They will add a new ingredient. They will feed my unwanted rage.

How do I stop them? How do I stop it?

I want my life back.

October: Alone

My body is springing recklessly up and down, but the sleep doesn't want to come out of me. Not yet. I feel it is very early. My eyes won't open even for this obnoxious attack on my sacred sleep. The wild motion comes to a halt, but the attack is not yet over. Someone is pressing their body down on top of my stomach. Someone small. A moist, warm, peanut buttery, nauseating breath is seeping into my sleep parted lips. He burps.

"Jeffery!" my eyes burst open.

He's now rolling with laughter at the edge of my bed. My feet help him to find the floor. He's up quick, running circles in my room, leaping, shouting with glee, "Snow! Snow! Snow!" He's out my door.

I sit up, gagging out his burp. He is so gross. I must look. Is there really snow? I find my way down the stairs and discover Mom digging out the top shelf of the coat closet. Yup, it snowed. It snowed in here, anyway. Hats, gloves, scarves, boots, all over the floor. Jeffery is now at Mom's feet, boinging up and down. I'm glad it's her turn to deal with him, but even more glad that I have missed out on him eating breakfast. Smelling it was bad enough. Listening to it would have killed me. At least, for a good part of my morning it would have, as his smacking sounds would surely have lingered, repeating within my brain.

"Is there school?" I ask.

"No school! No school!" Great, I started him on another chant. He's now doing a dance, sticking out his butt, shaking it, wagging it, and waving his arms around in the air. I grab a piece of raisin bread and sprint back up the stairs to the safety of my own room. This time I lock the door.

It's too early to text Abby. I'm sure with her first frozen sighting she leaped right back into bed. Sometimes crazy Berkshire weather can be good—at least, for her it can be good. She doesn't have a bratty little brother to wake her up on snow days like me. And anyway, I'm not so sure she'd even answer me. Since the 'Adams Incident', she

and I have become somewhat estranged. I don't know if it was her doing or my own—probably both. She really is my only good friend at school, my best friend, but still, there's no way I'd chance telling her about what has been going on up inside my head, the rage. She couldn't possibly understand that. I can hardly even understand it. And just me talking about what my head feels like makes her slanted eyes turn sideways; she knows when there is something more. She

knows that I am not telling all, that it's not "just a headache". There's no getting around Abby.

So that probably is why she hasn't texted or called me back in over a week; even our Facebook messages have turned void. Ever since I ran out of Mrs. Adams' class. I don't know, maybe I shouldn't have shut her out. Maybe it is time I let her in. Or maybe not. Either way, today I will get a hold of her. I have never felt so alone.

I send her a text. She'll get it when she wakes up. I hope she writes back. Or calls. Or just shows up at my house like old times...

My thoughts are disrupted. Someone's trying to get in my room. "Jessica, open your door." It's Dad.

"What?"

"No, open your door right now. What did I tell you about locking it?"

Hopefully his tongue has not yet met his teeth. I bound for the door, racing his quick temper. Luckily, I won. His teeth are partially exposed through his lips, keeping his tongue in its proper, safe place. Unfortunately, just the thought of his sound has made my temple flare. I rub my head along my hairline, hoping my obvious discomfort doesn't ignite his. He pretends not to notice my 'headache'.

"I rescheduled your appointment with Lisa. The roads are bad and your mother doesn't like to drive on them. Your appointment will be next Wednesday, the 2nd, after school. Ok?"

"Oh, yeah. Ok." That makes two appointments for next week. Neurologist on Tuesday, Lisa on Wednesday. Oh, joy.

I peer into his green eyes, mirror images of my own, just a shade lighter. Only his have crows-feet engraved off to their sides, sandy colored play dough skin that birds' feet have dipped into, leaving behind their perpetual mark. The play dough has dried, aged, grown out of its elastic, soft youth. Now, only little wrinkle-prints give hint of the once youthful smiles that once escaped those thin lips, creasing the sandy play dough skin that had been carefully fashioned around the green eyes. I have yet to encounter the mysteriously missing smiles that used to reside within his crow's feet face. They did once exist. Occasionally they still do. They existed when I was small. They exist when I am not home. When he's alone with Mom and Jeffery. All the old and new family photos say so.

We stand awkwardly for a moment, face to face. "Well, ok, I'm going to work."

"Ok. Bye Dad." I'm relieved to shut the door. He seems equally relieved to leave my room. I wait to hear him pull out of the driveway before I re-twist the lock.

The day drags on. I spend it locked in my room with my iPod blasting in my ears; my personal Jeffery defense. No, my noise defense.

Abby never responds. I never leave my room. I am alone. All day.

Un-enraged, but alone.

November

Life outside is dead: the trees, the leaves on the ground, the grass, the dirt. All the same color, all the same cold. No birds hop along. No bugs flutter by. No squirrels racing around a limb—dead—cold—emp- ty—alone. Only the silence is welcomed by me. But even that cannot last; it will end, too, and then all will die. My ears. My thoughts. My brain. My sanity. Me. Me. Maybe it should be me.

Mom's shadow is closing in on my feet. "Jess! Let's go!"

I pull my body up off the front steps. She's already in the car. I can see her impatience. We don't speak as she drives us farther and farther away from home. I think that this is a waste of time; she hopes that it isn't. She's tapping the steering wheel with what's left of her chewed up fingernails. My ears are focusing in. They are listening. Listening

to the tapping. Repeating the tapping over and over; tapping out the rhythm on their own personal drums. Tapping over the tapping. They won't stop. It won't stop. She won't stop. My eyes are glaring. Just stop! My brain is screaming. Screaming at Mom. Screaming at her nails. Screaming. Tapping. My fingers are pushing deep inside too-thin ear holes. The walls around my nails are screaming their pain. Pain that is abruptly good. Pain that is overtaking sound. Victory pain.

I am a mess as we step out of the car. Mom's eyes are bewildered as my raging eyes detonate into hers. She looks away. My heart goes down under, drowning deep inside my gut. What is wrong with me?

I follow her into the depths of the Medical Arts Complex. She leads the way, following the signs to Dr. Langer's office. Dr. Langer is a neurologist; mom says he's one of the best. I secretly hope that she's right.

Dr. Langer gives a thudding knock before entering the room. His chest is where his head should be. Strawberry blond hair stretches for the sun, or rather, light bulb. His blueberry eyes win the prize for extra plump. His smile: jumbo marshmallow surprise.

He is gigantic. Jack and the Beanstalk gigantic. His hand envelops mine, and then mom's in a shake. It is the first time I have smiled in over a month. I feel giddy. His enormous being has swallowed, in one gulp, both my tapping rage and my lingering remorse.

He's asking me what brings me here. Mom is answering him, not me. She's telling him something about my headaches. Words try to take form from behind my lips but they move much too slowly. Mom, though—her mouth is quick, and her eyes don't bother to look at mine as her mouth moves to fill in the blanks.

Not anymore. Not since we got out of the car. The sting of guilt is returning. A vision of my flaming eyes igniting into hers flashes through my brain.

"Well then, Jessica." Dr. Langer hunches down to give me a closer look when he's finished listening to Mom's lengthy ramble about all my recent 'issues'. "Let's take a peek!" He checks both ears and

down my throat; listens to my heartbeat; listens more for my lungs to expand and deflate. Turns out the light, asks for guilt ridden eyes to follow his flashlight left and right. Turns on the light and says, "Looking good!" Surely he needs a brighter light.

Then comes his list of questions: At what age did the headaches begin? How often do I have them? How long do they last? Do I feel them coming on? What kind of tingling? Do I experience a visual aura as well? And so on, and so on. His list of questions is as large as his gigantic body. He checks off Mom's, and occasionally my own answers one by one on his list. I hope that this is his only list. I wonder if it will ever end.

After way too much talking, he talks some more. He explains to me that he feels that I am experiencing migraine headaches. I do not both- er to explain to him that I feel that he is wrong. Actually, that I know that he is wrong. Not even he, "one of the best," seems to be able to understand what is really happening deep inside my brain. I may not know much, but I do know that a simple migraine headache could not possibly inflict the type of raging pain that explodes inside my brain day after day.

"As for medication, you have three options," he goes on. "Each one has originally been created to treat something else, but, we have found that each one, in different people, works wonders for treating migraines as well. The first medication is one that was created for pre- venting seizures. The second, for lowering blood pressure. The third, for depression."

Then he starts up another new and

lengthy speech about how all medications have their own side effects and that some medications work better than others depending on the person, but if one doesn't work, I can go on to try the next. I want to tell him that I have no intention of trying any medication for migraine headaches, especially one that was made for something else, and that I won't be made into his own personal guinea pig, but that would only open way for even more talk. I just nod and agree so that I can leave soon.

After spending what seems like the entire, stretched out, never ending morning in Dr. "Jack and the Beanstalk" Langer's office, me and my prescription-flapping mom are finally out the door. She decides to bring me straight to school, since I've already "missed out on enough time this morning." But I wish I could miss out on the entire day, or better yet, the entire year. What's the point of returning?

Yet here I am once again, walking through school doors, ears wide open and awaiting their certain, never failing death. I gradually trudge to my first stop, signing in at the office. Here my eyes are met with the unexpected. Well, really I should have expected it. There he is, pushing back the silk from his eyes, the better to see me with, and smiling his devious smile, the better to devour me with Brandon. Of course he's here. Most likely waiting his daily turn to 'visit' Mr. Owens. I can only imagine what he's in for this time. I don't smile back.

"Well, you've made it just in time for lunch, Jessica." Miss Jackson blinks through her thick owl glasses, her lips, tight, forming their who-who? beak like an 'O'. I hand her my note from Mom. She blinks again, fluttering me away with her stubby wing fingers, "You're all set. Go on now."

Brown wolf eyes follow as I turn for the door. My hands push the heavy metal bar, exposing the way for my body to meet its school-induced doom. My feet move mindlessly down the hall. My eyes don't bother to take notice of their surroundings, but my ears have become alerted. They are met with a familiar sound. Laughter. Abby's laugh- ter. I feel my head lifting up, eyes forcing their green globes to clear and focus in. She's heading my way, although she doesn't seem to no- tice me. She's walking with Rochelle, laughing; apparently she's found her new 'BFF'. I want to look away, but I can't—my eyes have become magnetized. And Rochelle's eyes have met mine. Her smile twists into a scowl. Her elbow is jabbing Abby's side. As though I can't see her.

Hazel ovals meet hazy green ones. Lips pause. I feel Abby's words about to form, but then fade away. Ovals roll. Head turns. Mouth laughs. She is gone.

I am alone. Alone with wet goopy eyes, standing in the middle of a hallway with people pushing and shoving by me from all sides, moving all around me, walking past me in every direction. I have no direction. But someone gives me a direction. Someone is grabbing my hand and pulling me, pulling me away, pulling fast.

"Come on!" I am caught by the wolf with black-silk hair. He is running me down the hall and out the school doors. Grasping, pulling me. His grip loosens up as mine is gives in. We're running, holding each other's hands. Why? I yank free and stop. We're outside, alone. Face to face. Sharp white teeth grin down at me.

"Come on," Brandon says again. This time I have a choice. My hands are free. I look back at school doors; they do not invite me back in. I release my fate into his canine claws. I grab his hand letting him take the lead. We run and run.

Finally, we stop. We've passed the football field and the tree that once comforted me. We're deep in the woods, standing face to face on a thinly ventured, rough path. "You came with me?" his voice is al- most a whisper. I feel my shoulders shrug and the red of my exhausted cheeks thicken. My hand lifts his to his chest.

"You're still holding my hand." My voice barely reaches his ears.

Squinty brown eyes tease my green ones. We both let go.

"Let me show you something," he turns back around, ready to lead me farther into the woods. My stomach turns, deep down inside. An inborn instinct for safety; my feet will not follow him any further.

"I have to go back," I hear my voice tell him. His canine being senses my fear.

"It's ok. It's not like that." Wolf eyes search mine, "It's just some- thing that I made. A secret—you'll like it."

He puts out his hand.

I make no response. I barely even know him, other than the fact that he is trouble.

My body has become that of a threatened deer. Sudden stiffness overcomes me, and I cannot move, I cannot speak. My silence has spoken. He hears.

"Hey, it's ok. I'll bring you back. Come on." Wolf teeth transform back to human teeth. Devious eyes un-squint and lighten. He's careful not to touch me. I feel my body begin to relax.

"No, it's ok. Show me."

His eyes smile as he takes the lead again, this time more slowly.

His hands keep to his sides except to push back the brush that grows thickly into our rugged path. We've already walked for at least five minutes and all I have seen is more and more trees, roots, prickers and leafless twigs. The path, already claustrophobic, is beginning to squeeze in around us more and more as we head on, single file, farther and farther away from school. Jagged rocks are taking form under our feet as the ground gradually inclines upward. I wonder if we are lost.

"Over here," he says, stopping suddenly, my un-anticipating body smacking into his. I feel his warmth passing through his thick, hooded sweatshirt, through my own coat, and into my body as his arm wraps around me, catching me as we collide. I hadn't realized just how cold I've been until now. Brandon points through a small opening in the trees at something that I don't see.

"Come on." His body bounds forward, leaping over and around rocks and prickly twigs. I try to keep up. Luckily for me, we are really, finally here.

What I see next is amazing, something I almost didn't see. Right in front of me, in the middle of nowhere, stands a tree house. Well, it's not exactly in a tree, but it has the form, the size, the structure of a perfect little tree house sitting on the ground. I run my hand around the ridged, slivery sides until I find the door. Brandon follows me in- side and shuts the door. We have disappeared; there are no windows. Only a bird might discover us through some little peep hole up in the roof. It is dark. I feel Brandon's hand brush up against my leg. Then there is light—he has lit an old lantern. I can't help the sigh of relief that escapes my lips, and he can't help the glow of the lantern that exposes his mischievous grin.

We sit facing each other on the

treehouse's only chair, a log. I bring my feet up to my butt and hug my knees in tight. Our eyes meet. They whisper their secrets across the darkened silence. A warmth is rising up underneath the skin of my cheeks. I feel my lips as they shape into a smile, and his lips imitate mine. My green eyes shy down underneath thick lashes: I feel the hunger of his brown ones. My words interrupt our unspoken language.

"Why'd you rescue me from the mad stampede?"

He shrugs and smiles.

My tongue keeps silent my real question: Why me?

Our silence returns, but it's not complete silence. Not this time.

The light has gone out from behind green eyes... His hand has found a stick. A small stick that he is tapping; tapping on the log beneath his hip. I try to push away the sound, push that tapping from my thoughts. I try to push it away from my brain but it taps it's way right back. The more I push that tapping out, the more it comes back in.

Now my eyes decide they want to join the fun—they start to focus in: in on his stick, in on his hand, squeezing themselves shut and then popping back open again. They let the sound in, as my ears do. I need to shut it out, for my rage has begun to swell…

I can't. It is all too much. I am going to snap. No. I am going to snap his stick.

I am the rage of lightning. The snap is within my fist—a sharp prick under my hand. Brandon's stick is snapped to bits. It's held inside his hand, the hand wrapped beneath my fist. I feel the slice of skin.

Wolf eyes are coiling into mine; I feel his overpowering grip eliminating my own; his fingers peel mine off of his. But he will not release the hand—my hand that has assaulted his. I feel the squeezing pain; it burns me with his strength.

But even more I feel the release of my own stormy rage. It has struck and diffused in a matter of seconds. Newfound agony revives my strange sanity, for his tapping is done.

His smile is also done. I feel my quick pulse through the pressure he keeps on my hand. I feel his rage ripping me apart through dark, howling, cold eyes. His body rises up but his eyes hold me down. I can't look away. I can't move. I'm afraid of what he might do. Of what he might say.

Finally, my eyes allow themselves to look away, down to the darkness of the dirt floor. I feel his grip loosening. He examines my bleeding hand.

"It's just a scrape," he gets me to look back up. Up into cold eyes. "I'm sorry," my voice is quivery. It speaks my shame.

His silence awaits an explanation, but I have none. My mouth re- mains shut.

"Come on. I'll bring you back." The sound in his voice echoes the cold message within his eyes.

The trail he takes is an awkward path back. I wish I had never come. If he didn't think I was crazy before, he certainly does now.

We're almost at my tree. I see it approaching quickly up ahead. I grab his hand; one last chance to reclaim my sanity and save our unexpected, half-formed friendship. Brandon stops. He turns to look at me, the first time our eyes have met since we left his little tree house that sits on the ground.

"I'm really sorry, Brandon," I have found my voice.

Squinty brown eyes peer down at me from behind his silky black curtain. He pushes my wild locks of hair out of the way, exposing timid, moist green eyes. He looks closer. I feel the prickly chills shoot down the back of my neck and into my spine as his lips turn slightly up; a sweet smile. He keeps my hand in his, gently, as we walk back to school doors. Together we push through them.

*

There's an unsettling rumble in the depths of my gut. It's not so much from the sketchy excuse I rambled out while entering class, just as everyone else was packing up their books to leave, or from the shot of mistrust that reamed out of my teacher's eyes as her ears picked up on my jabbering lie. It's not even the venom spurting from her tongue and thick red lips, lashing out her justifiable doubt. It's something else; it's something much worse. It comes from the beginning of my day—no, from the beginning of months ago. I have made myself alone, I have kept everyone out. I keep everyone out.

So why did I let him in? Brandon. Just his name makes my rum- bling swoosh. I don't want to push him away, but I know it will hap- pen. The sounds will inflict my rage again. And again he will witness my unpredictable, crazed being, one that I cannot control. One that I hate. Me.

November: The Day After Yesterday

Cold, dense bricks push against my back. A swarming buzz of voices surrounds and flies by. The clouds disperse, filling the yellow mounds that await them. They are gone. I let my back slide down until my butt hits the ground. I wish Mom would hurry up. Soon the teachers will be on their way out, too. My hands move to rub my aching ears; their insides should be bleeding. How else could I survive an entire day? All I can do is sit in the shadows of classroom corners, head crumpling down, fingernails twisting, shoving deep inside my cursed ears, ears wallowing in their pain. They deserve it. I wish they would die. For with their death, I might survive.

Finally, she is here. And she's happy, I'm sure. It's Wednesday and time to meet Lisa. I can imagine her skipping me to the door, handing me over with her huge, golden-toothed smile, and waiting for the fairy tale cure. Yeah, right.

Lisa takes in earful after earful, overflowing scoops of Mom's out- sider's perspective on me. But I don't care. I am nowhere near here; I have already heard Mom's story once too many times, with every new

doctor that we see. Not one will be able to lay their pointing finger down on the truth, for what is the truth? Does it even exist? Is there even such a thing…? Girl hears click; click forms rage; girl explodes!

…Maybe they will label me as the first, real life, living time bomb

… "Can she be defused!?"

Mom has left the room, leaving just me and Lisa. We sit staring at each other, each waiting for the other to speak.

She smiles, "It's ok if you don't feel like talking. I have no problem with just hanging out." She turns to her desk and puts down her note- pad and pen. She begins reaching and digging deep into her drawer for something. Then she turns with a deck of cards and a smile.

"You like Solitaire?" she asks.

Her hands pull over a small, round coffee table, setting it between us. She doesn't seem to notice or care that I haven't replied. Her thumbs slowly begin to let the cards fall, sticky clumps, mixing together from the left and the right; a lazy shuffle. With each plop of the cards she spices them back up with a perfect backbend that flutters down like an old-fashioned flip book. She taps the deck down twice, hard, aligning the cards just right in between each new shuffle. It doesn't matter about her backbend technique; the cards remain clumped and stuck together anyway. I watch now as she begins to line the cards out: seven across, first one flipped. Six more across top, second one flipped, and so on. Neither one of us attempts a word.

Lisa begins studying the cards: she moves the Queen of Hearts on top of the King of Spades. The 2 of Clubs moves on top of the 3 of Hearts. She stops to think. It's taking way too long.

"7 of hearts. You have a black 8." Lisa's lips smile.

"Oh, thanks." She moves the 7 and flips the card underneath it, tapping the table twice with the tips of her fingers.

"Your mom seems pretty worried about you." her voice is direct, but her eyes never sway from her game.

"I guess."

She studies her cards some more. And some more.

"Nope, you're stuck. Pick from your deck," I say, trying to move her game along.

She picks a black 3 and sets it down, frowning. She taps her fingers once more, twice.

My ears cue in.

"She does talk a lot," Lisa says. Her eyes glance up with her words, away from the cards.

"Uh, yeah."

She goes back to her game, flipping a new card from her deck. It's the Ace of Spades. Lisa places it above the others.

Her fingers tap twice. Again. I feel my temple flare.

"Is what she says true?" Lisa is looking right at me now, "I mean, about you?

My shoulders shrug.

I wait for the next double tap. It doesn't come, but my eyes glare at her offending fingertips anyway.

"Is there a bathroom in here?"

She points to my escape and I'm quickly on my way. Out.

I splash water into my eyes and over my

face. I can't let myself lose it in front of her. I have to remain calm. Sane. She seems ok, other than her annoying finger-tapping habit. If I can just deal with it for

a little bit longer, I'll be able to leave. I give myself one more good splash before walking back in to re-expose my quickly triggered brain to her tappity-tap finger tips.

She's still studying her card lineup as I return.

"Well, I think this game is done. What do you think?"

I sit down and give the cards a quick look-over, "Yeah, it's done."

She smiles, "And, that's about all the time that we have for today." I almost smile, too.

Mom's called back in. I feel the tension in her left eye as it twitches a little. I can sense that she really wants to know what was said, but also knows that she's not allowed to. Lisa can't tell her anything with- out my consent first; our conversation is officially "confidential," the same as Ms. Shay had told me. But anyway, would Mom really want to know that all we did was play cards, and that the only conversation (if you can call it that) was about her?

Before we leave, Mom schedules my next one-hour session with Lisa for two weeks from today, a Wednesday. This next appointment will be just the two of us, alone for one whole hour. Mom will not be entering the room. Maybe she won't be liking Lisa after all…

*

When we arrive home, Dad is awaiting our return out on the front steps, his cigarette clenched between two tight lips. He flicks it onto the dead, brown grass of our yard as we step out of the car. October's freak snow came and left without a trace, leaving the grass to freeze and die. Mom's eyebrows grimace in annoyance; her eyes become the flare of his smoking cigarette butt that lies teasing the ground. She smothers it with her shoe and calls him a "fire hazard just waiting to happen."

SOUND

I try to slip inside, but Dad's voice is trailing in close behind me, "There's a message on the machine for you—some boy." His feet are practically on top of mine.

My heart skips as I redirect my path straight to the phone. It has to be Brandon. Then I stop. Jeffery is sitting on the floor one foot away from the TV, watching Tom and Jerry and chewing on Dad's home- made beef jerky. From across the room I can see the corners of his lips opening and shutting, chewing in his disgusting way. I can't hear the smacking yet, but it doesn't matter; the tingling has already begun. I refuse to let the sound waves reach my ears. I turn dead in my tracks, ready to bound up the stairs, but instead, I bound right into Dad. I forgot he was there—right there, at my feet. And it is his foot that I step on.

His agitated voice yelps his toes' pain. His tongue sucks his teeth.

My temple explodes its sudden rage. My eyes bulge, blasting green lightning. They zap his gritting lips.

"What are you doing?" Dad's voice demands a response.

I look down, away from his fizzling-out sound. My rage subsides; the sound is gone.

"Sorry, Dad, I...I just forgot something." This time, I successfully bound around him and up the stairs.

I shut my door quickly, debating whether to lock it or not. Dad might be on his way up right now, following me to my room. I wait a minute. He doesn't show, so I chance my luck and twist the lock tightly. Now there really is no way to call Brandon back. I don't have his number, and the only caller ID in the house is the one on the phone downstairs, right next to Jeffery's smacking.

I feel my stomach churn, an acidic whirlpool of stress. Even if I could call Brandon back, I know that a relationship with him could never last. It doesn't matter that I've been avoiding him for the past few weeks, looking at him as though he is some sort of preying beast, for now even the thought of a relationship with him brings me to consider the person that I should really fear—the one right here, right deep down inside of me. For it is me. Is there anyone else who cannot tolerate other people's sounds, turning into an instant inferno from just the slightest noise? Is there any other person who, in their right mind, whips a dish across the room because someone was chewing their food loudly, even if the one chewing is annoying and gross? Who else would really care if someone was tapping their fingers, or a little innocent stick? Me. Just me.

Somewhere in my brain the wires must be crossed, the lining wearing thin, tempting little sparks to ignite. With each sound, the wires thicken, expand, their thinned linings grind together, and their sparks veer into flames—shooting flames, raging inside my brain. I have become a beast, so it is better that I don't call Brandon back. Ever.

The pressure in my head builds thickly with each new thought, forcing the waterfall out of my green eyes. The water flows down the hills, over my pink cheeks, and through the crevices of stone-parted lips. There is no sound. The flow is a silent downward stream, revealing what it is to be alone, truly alone. I want to die.

I fumble with the lock on my door; it opens. I don't wipe the flow from my cheeks. My feet take me down the hall and into Mom and Dad's room. They are not there. I pick up Mom's address book from her nightstand. I find the loose phone card for the Crisis Center. My fingers lift the phone and dial. Someone answers; wants to know if they can help me. I say I want to die. Please, just let me die.

*

Mom and Dad have left me here, me and my little sorted bag of clothes. I am brought to a room with two beds: one for me and one for, whoever 'she' is. I have passed through the long hall containing other teens like me, at least they look like me: normal on the outside, most likely deranged within. Some are just sitting, alone, on a bench or chair. Others are in the rec-room, playing ping-pong or watching TV. I only see my room for a brief moment, because the doctors want to meet with me now. Right now.

I'm led off through the great hallway and into a windowless room, closed in, squeezed down, at a cluttered, high desk with two doctors. Both hold clipboards and pens. They study my eyes, my expressions, my voice, my every move and gesture. They ask me why I want to die, if I use drugs or alcohol, about the sounds, how long this has been going on, if I've hurt myself or anyone else before; more and more. They check and scribble down all that I say do. This is the first time that

I have allowed myself to tell the truth, the whole truth. Right here. Right now. Now, in the hands of those who could take away the rest of my life: lock me up, send me away, drug me until I am numb, drug me until I am dumb. I don't care, either way. If I died in their hands it would be ok. As long as they can take away my rage.

The doctors tell me they feel I am experiencing social anxiety and depression. In the morning they will test me further with a complete blood test and a thorough psychological evaluation, but I don't know what good it will do. They're concerned about my anger, but still they've managed to distort all that I have said. "Your emotional response to these different sounds is triggered by an already existing anxiety." They're wrong. My "anxiety" is my emotional response, it is my rage. Rage that is triggered by sounds. My personal equation: sound plus ears equals rage. But there's no point in arguing this to the doctors; their minds are already made up. So what was the point

in telling them the truth, anyway? I guess I really didn't have to worry about doctors thinking I'm crazy after all. I mean, I've laid it all out: the unpredictable, instant brain cyclone, lashing upward, twisting through my brain, escaping through poison eyes, wild hands, and fleeing feet; my psychotic, anomalous rage.

They don't care. The sooner they can stamp me with their book-concocted labels, the sooner they can send me out and on my way—drugged, and on my way.

For now, the doctors are working on getting my parents' consent to start me on medication for depression, due to my "suicidal tendencies". They talk to Mom on the phone. She tells them, "Yes, do what- ever you need to do," and then she asks to talk to me. I tell them no. I have nothing to say. Really, I wouldn't know what to say. The shame is dripping, leaking into my already drenched brain. It doesn't matter what the doctors here think of me, or the other kids. But my Mom?

And Dad. I push away all thoughts of what he must be thinking of me. I can sense his tongue suctioning his teeth, all the way from here. My hand rubs my temple fiercely.

I stop. All the doctors are looking at me. "What are you feeling, Jessica?" one asks. "Nothing," I lie. I want to be alone

"You were rubbing your head pretty

hard."

"I'm ok now."

Surprisingly, they let me go. They're apparently done with me for today. I walk by a small, lingering crowd of two girls and one boy.

Seemingly they're waiting for me, for it is after me that their eyes slowly trail. I pretend not to notice. My head shifts down. I move along, down the hall and into my room (well, I guess technically 'our' room). I'm glad no one follows. I'm glad she's not here.

I feel my body collapsing, fully dressed, on top of my so-called bed. On top of a scratchy old blanket. I feel it lurking underneath my cheek. Polyester. My skin repulses, and I tear it out rapidly from under me, right off the bed. It lies in a heap on the floor, in company with my twisted sanity, for all to see. But no one does see. I ripped my pain out from deep inside of me; I spread it out for them to see. But they did not see. Instead, they stuffed it right back inside of me and covered it up. Hid it deep within me, for me to bear alone. Again. Deep in my dark insanity.

November: Coming Home

I am the autumn leaf set free from the tree. The nutrients rising up from my mother's veins, nutrients that have flowed from her veins and into mine, have been cut off, leaving me to die a deliberate death. At first, I tried to block away her nourishment. But then, as I realized that the flow had ceased, I wanted to cling back. I flamed out the colors of my final fight for life, a life I once thought I'd be better off living on my own. Only now I realize that I no longer have that choice; hanging on will not save me. So I let loose. I spiral down with the wind in search of solid ground. I am no longer a part of the tree, for in my death I become my own. I have struggled, altered, and died in my making. Now the ground is my only hope for resurrection, the resurrection of a new me. My body will decompose into the frozen ground, underneath the layers of soon-to-be snow. My life will be forgotten, overlooked. I am the one crazy leaf that tried to hold on—to hold onto things that weren't there anymore: her mother's strength, her fellow leaves, her wind-blown sanity. If she rises up in the Spring, will she take on a new form? Or will her body become that of the ground in which she will lay for so long?

I'm coming home. I'm coming home on my own. Alone. I'm set- ting out on my own path, apart from my mother. Her words will not speak for me anymore: I will speak my own voice, my own story. My own blood will flow through my veins. No more doctors will hear her words over mine—not this time, not anymore. If I have learned any- thing in this past week it is who I am, or rather, who I'm not. I'm not one who should let someone else talk for me just so

I can escape a bit more quickly. I am not one who should wear a label just so a doctor can pat himself on the back. All that those doctors say is untrue; they don't know; they don't understand what is happening in the tangled depths of my brain. But I know that it is happening, that it is real. I feel it every day. Doctors cannot help me, yet they refuse to let me die. That is, they refuse to let my heart stop beating, for in soul I am already dead. I live in Hell, for all I feel is pain.

So, I think, so what if I am crazy? No one else seems to know it except me. In these past days I've watched as, one by one, those around me were stamped, labeled, bookmarked, and inscribed into their 'proper' places; drugged into their medically approved dazes and sent on their way. They were each filed, one by one, into a great book of names. But me, I am a secret. I'm their crumpled up, scribbled-on piece of paper; I don't fit into their book. Sure, my symptoms match some of what they know. I mean, I am depressed; I did wish to die, and I do get anxious. But even so, even though I am not-fully-diagnosable, they point to the names in their book. So here they are, the names that they have given to me: depression and social anxiety. But that's all that they are able to recognize in me. They have stamped me, labeled me, stuck me in their book. They've given me drugs that I have pretended to take, and now they can send me on my way. My way. I don't care what they have to say; I am starting anew, by myself. I will rise up from my mental death. I will explore on my own what it is that lashes up my ear canals, entering and erupting my brain, creating my self-destructive rage. I will find the answer on my own. Alone. Just me. Just me.

Mom and Dad are here. They're here taking me and my small, dirty bag of clothes home. Mom's lips smile their "it's going to be ok" smile. But Dad's lips tightly frown the truth, the truth of what our lives are about to become, or rather of what they have already become. Only now we can no longer pretend that our lives haven't changed.

That our family hasn't. that I haven't. And it's all because of me; our lives will never again be the same. All because of me.

Riding home, we are hijacked by a silent awkwardness, trapped in- side our four metal and glass walls. Hostages in each other's presence. Not one of us has the words to break free from our silence, but finally Mom speaks.

"Your doctors seem to think that you'll be ok, Jessica, as long as you continue seeing Lisa and taking your medication."

"Oh," is all I manage to say.

There is no point in letting her know that I plan to fight on my own from here on out, that I will create my own plan in defiance of what the doctors say. Because they are wrong—I am not ok. I will not be ok, not until I find out what is really going on. I will follow along with their plan of meeting with Lisa, and I will continue pretending to take their drugs, but I will do it only to keep them off my back. Their words will become to me like the torturous sounds they make are to them—nothing. Their voices will form from within their mouths, depart through their teeth and lips, transform into flowing air waves, and pass through my brain like a gentle breeze; they will not affect me. And as for their opinions? Well, they can just blow away... Poof!

An enormous smile is waiting for me out on the front steps as we arrive home. I'm relieved to find that this mouth—Jeffery's mouth— is frozen shut in its smiling position rather than in its normal position of wide-open smacking, stuffed with food as I usually find it. With this frozen-faced but bumbling figure appears the familiar smile of Mari- ana, our neighbor and (apparently) our family's newfound babysitter. Her arm rests above Jeffery's shoulders, seemingly holding him down, for his body is bouncing up and down underneath her arm. Mariana's arm doesn't budge until she sees my feet hit the ground and our eyes meet. My lips turn up into a sudden and unexpected smile. I'm glad to be home—it's strange, but I truly am.

Jeffery almost tackles me to the ground. His arms wrap around my waist and squeeze me skinny.

"You're home! You're home!" He really can't survive a day without a good, hyper chant, can he? My eyes meet his deep, dark brown ones, the reincarnation of Grandpa's eyes. Whenever our eyes happen to meet, I feel I could almost love him for a splinter of a second. I hug him back, but then peel him away.

"I'm going to go wash my clothes," I say, flinging my dirty 'escape' bag of clothes over my shoulder and making a quick exit. No one bothers to stop me. I'm on my own.

Once my clothes are in the wash I head up to my room. It's strangely clean—too clean. Mom must have been busy while I was gone. I'm sure she searched my entire room. For what I don't know, but I really don't care; there was nothing for her to find. But now there is something for me to find: the big heap of books on top of my bed. School books. Ugh. Not only was Mom cleaning my room, but she was also cleaning out my school locker, collecting all of my week-behind assignments. As if I will ever catch up. How can I, when I was already behind before all this happened? Today is Wednesday, so tomorrow is Thursday. I hope they don't expect me to go straight back to school, but somehow, I'm sure that they do.

*

They do. Here I go again, back to school. We're heading in late, arms full of books, Mom and I. Before I can go back to class I have to meet with my guidance counselor, Mrs. Peters, along with a parent.

She wants to talk about my grades, and I'm sure, about much more… Unfortunately, she does. Mrs. Peters is giving Mom an earful about

how my past few months in class have been going: head on desk, unprepared, not paying attention, barely passing tests, and border- line-failing just about every class.

Mom's face is growing grim. Is it possible for the tips of her eye- brows to reach the point of her nose? Her expression is that of a crazed chicken-hawk, and I have just become her prey. Her eyes narrow in, her beak opens wide, ready to screech out my final moment of life. Then she stops, as though she has just remembered something. That she is actually human? No. Just everything that has been going on; everything that's been going on with me. That is exactly what be- gins to squawk out from her beak-turned lips: all about me. My wanting to die. My being admitted into the psychiatric unit. My depression. I don't bother to stop her. What's the point? Maybe Mrs. Peters will convince my teachers to give me a break. Who knows?

Mrs. Peters agrees to talk with my teachers about giving me extra time to complete the work that I have missed, but she's not so sure that there's anything more that she can do. However, she does suggest that I take time to visit the school psychiatrist,

Mr. Rolland, from time to time when I need help. I just nod and agree. There's nothing that he can do for me. I'll deal on my own.

Finally, Mom and I are set free. She helps me to return my books to my locker and then we head out on our separate ways: Mom to go back home, and I to face the horror of entering first period late after missing a full week of school, and, I'm sure, to find Abby sitting in the very front row as if she's just waiting to be the very first witness of my discomfited return.

Yes, there she is sitting up front, pen in hand. Normally slant- ed eyes are un-slanted and wide—staring directly at me. I feel her two bulging eyes as they follow me to the back of the room. Her eyes, along with the eyes of everyone else in the class. The teacher, hand out, asks me for my late slip. I'm glad that she has followed me all the way to my seat. I don't think that I could have handled re-walking the catwalk of eyeballs all the way back to her desk. I hand my note to her, wait for her to proceed back to the front of the room, and then collapse my head onto its old familiar place upon the wood of my desk.

The day drags on as if I had never been gone from school. Class to class I sit in the back, head on my desk, digging my fingernails deep into two aching ear-holes. I'm not sure who avoids the other more, Abby or me. But it really doesn't matter; we have officially and intentionally gone on our separate ways. She has Rochelle, and I have my new friend 'Rage.'

As for the other friend that I've left intentionally without a trace, I haven't seen him yet. Brandon. I haven't seen him all day. I guess I shouldn't be so surprised; he's probably skipping class, enduring in-house suspension, or expelled. What was I thinking anyway, going with him the other day? He's always in trouble. Even in just our one day together we managed to leave school grounds in the middle of the day. What kind of couple would we even make, his mischief and my rage? I'd surely be in constant trouble and have to visit Mr. Owens' office every day. No way! Then why does his vision continue to haunt me? His hand holding mine; his eyes, brown like a wolf's, searching deep into my green ones. His smile. His voice. Him. Him. I need to find him…

I feel my feet carrying me. They're carrying me away from the bus that is supposed to bring me back home. Away from the front of the school. They're carrying me around back, across a football field, past a familiar tree and onto a rugged path. I'm running—tripping, following a narrowly explored path deep into the woods. The home of the wolves. The home of the wolf.

Where is he?

I have found his little tree house that sits on the ground. My hand runs along the side, feeling the rough, splintery sides until I find the door. My eyes close. I feel the cold air expanding deep within my lungs.

Why am I here?

My hands push the door open; he is not

there. Now there is nothing that can stop the tears from coming. I want him here—I want him here to hold me in his arms and tell me that it's ok, that I'm ok. To tell me that I don't have to be alone, that he will stand beside me no matter what, that he can still love the person that I have become.

I want to know that he sees me, the me that still lives somewhere inside of this body, the me that grabbed his hand and didn't let him go another step further until he knew that I was sorry. I am sorry. I am so sorry for everything.

An hour must have passed, for the sun is going down. I will never find my way out of here now. I am stuck alone in the middle of the woods, in the wolf's den. I'm sure Mom is already getting worried. Dad's tongue will soon begin sucking his teeth. For sure he's on his way home, and he won't find me there; he'll find Mom pacing back and forth, babbling about where I could possibly be. They'll call Abby. She'll say "sorry, she doesn't know". But she won't be sorry, for what does she care? She doesn't care about me.

I feel the tears starting up again behind my already swollen eyes. But they don't fall—not this time, for something stops them. Something else is here. Fear. Something is moving outside. I hear a crunch on the crisp ground, too loud—too loud to be something small like a squirrel.

A raccoon? A deer? A bear?! I grasp the door and shut it tight; my only source of light is gone. I can't move to find the old lantern. I don't want to breathe a sound, so I try to hold my breath. Whatever it is, it is here. Right here. Right on the other side of these thin wooden walls. The door bursts open.

"Jessica!"

Before I even realize what has happened I feel my body leaping into the air and my arms wrapping around Brandon's neck. My feet are off the ground. He catches me; he's holding me. His breath is hot, seeping into my hair. Brandon. My tears let loose.

As my feet hit the ground the warmth of

his hands tilts up my swollen cheeks. I can't see his brown eyes, but I know they are there. Their message passes through the dark. He is here. He draws me back in, into the strength and safety of his arms. I am safe now. He is here.

His body persuades mine back inside the little house. He is sitting me onto the log. His hands draw in the light of the lantern and shut the door. Our lips don't speak, only our eyes. His eyes that search mine, as my own eyes search his. Our hands meet as we sit face to face on the log.

"Where were you?" He asks the question that had earlier been I want to tell him. I feel the words trying to take form; my lips are parting open, but then they close. My eyes find the ground. His hand finds my chin and his eyes bring mine back to his again. My body shivers. Fear. The fear of letting him in, the fear that he'll want 'out'. I should have taken my own advice—I should have stayed away, out of his sight. But now it's too late. We are here. He is here, here with me.

"Brandon," my voice escapes from behind my quivering lips, rupturing into a sudden flood of words. Words that gush out, creating the thick flow. "I didn't want you to know. I didn't want you to think I'm crazy." Tears are combining into the gushing words.

"Brandon, I'm sorry. I should have never come here. I'm sorr—" He's hushing me; hushing me with his lips. Soft, warm, moist, searching, quivering lips. Salty tears mix together, filling parted lips as they merge together: our first kiss. Brandon's warm hand, searching with his kiss, is discovering the skin of my back, crawling up under- neath my shirt, dissolving the hard layers of ice, melting it softly, engraving his print deep within my frozen being. Each muscle, one by one, releases its tight, frozen fear, relaxing up from the engraving in my back, down through my arms, and into my legs and feet. All that is left for me is his lips, his hands, the sensations his body sends through mine, tingling deeply into my core—that and the beating of our hearts.

Brandon's hand doesn't leave my back as our lips release. Our bodies never stop the pull, the pull that comes from somewhere down deep and gravitates us closer together. My head finds refuge on his chest. My eyes close, allowing my ears to listen more closely to the beating of his heart, which beats in rhythm with my own. My hands nestle their way up the back of his coat, exposing even more of his irresistible warmth. He is here—here with me. I am no longer alone.

"Do you trust me, Jess?" his voice seems to echo deep inside his chest. I slowly rub my head back and forth over the sound as it fades beneath my cheek.

"I do." My voice is only a whisper. I do trust him, I think. Only I'm scared of why he asks.

"Tell me what happened."

My head lifts off his chest. His hands embrace my face, creating a path for our eyes to meet.

"You trust me?" he repeats. Prickling chills

descend my back. Wolf eyes overtake me, springing across the path.

Yes, I want to say, but only my lips move my response; my voice doesn't exist.

Brandon waits for me to speak. He retains one hand on the side of my cheek, keeping my eyes in place; he will not let our connection break. A small drop of water escapes, trickling down from a green field across a glossy cheek, and absorbs into the strength of a hand. The hand turns soft, following the upward trail created by the water and finding the place where it escaped. It dries away the fear and pain that reside there.

Brandon pulls me back into his arms. My words escape.

I hear myself telling him about the sounds and the rage, about my family and school, about the doctors, what they say, and how I wished to die. And I speak about him, my fear of being close to him or close to anyone. I feel my words start to fade away.

A whisper asks him if he thinks I am crazy.

"No," is all he says. His arms have taken me back into their home. He holds me close, close to a fire that flames from within him from beneath his pulsing chest. His mouth searches through my tangled locks, searching and kissing what there is to be found underneath my tangled mess. My life has been poured out from my lips, into his ears, and now lingers inside his brain. He holds it there uncensored;

it now belongs to him. He is free to do with it what he wants: to hold it, expose it, twist it into his own, making up his own mind of what I am. I had come out of that institute alone, on my own, stronger than I was. For I had made my choice: I wanted to be alone (or so I tried to think). Now I am not alone; now I am with someone who I barely even know. I threw my body into his arms, but he caught me by my soul. He took it as it is, and now he knows all about me—who I am.

He knows the rage within my head. And yet, he's still holding me. He says that I'm not crazy…but I know the truth. He is so very wrong.

SOUND

It has gotten late. I don't know how long we have been here like this, holding each other in our arms, but it is late. I feel it from some internal clock ticking within. I pop up, out from the wrapped-up blanket of his arms.

"Brandon—my Mom!" I hear my voice ring. Reality is setting in. His eyes remain strangely calm as they look back into mine. "I'm going to be in so much trouble. I have to go home. Now."

His hand pushes the door open, exposing the blackness of night setting in.

I feel my mouth open, but my words are lost in a moonless, starless night. Green eyes dart out, reflecting the lantern's light. Reflecting the realization of being trapped in the night.

He shuts the door. His eyes grow thin. They are grinning into mine—teasing—grinning. Why do they change this way? Do you trust me? His question re-enters my mind; it's circling in my brain. Do you trust me? My body has begun to shake. My whispered answer is trying to reshape, I do…I do. But then why don't I feel that I do?

Brandon's mouth is forming a half-smile, large, sharp, wolf- shaped. My mind and body suddenly want me to escape—but to where? There is nowhere to escape.

Brandon is picking up on my fear. The teasing grin in his eyes clears as his lips tell me with their smile not to be afraid, "Hey, it's ok; I know the way out of here."

His hand reaches and pulls a phone out of his pocket. He places it calmly into my two shivering hands, "Call home. Let your mom know you're coming home."

My cheeks flush in shame. What made me think of him the way I had?

When I dial home, my fears are confirmed. Mom is mad, and so is Dad, she says. He is gone, out looking for me. I tell Mom that I missed the bus and that I didn't have my phone. That I was out walking, thinking, and lost track of time. That I met up with my friend, Brandon, but "he'll bring me home in a little while."

It's all true, right?

She tells me to call Dad. "Can't you?" I ask.

I can't bear to hear that sound. Please, won't you call?

She says she will, just this once, but that I better get home, "really, really soon."

Brandon leads out into the night by the light of his lantern, only on a different path than the one we took before. This path leads away from the school to the back of his house. He says that it's closer and the path is wider, that he used it when he was building his little house. He calls his sister, Sharron, as we make our way down the winding path. Sharron tells him that their dad is out with friends, but she doesn't mind giving me a ride home. He asks her to turn on their back light.

We have only walked a for few more minutes when I can make out a hint of light. The path is coming to an end and is quickly transforming into a small back yard with a little wooden deck growing off the back of a house. His house. Sharron is sitting out on the edge of the little deck, awaiting our return. A strange, illuminated smile lights her face. Her long hair is black as the night; it falls over thin shoulders, wrapping behind, blending in with the darkness.

"So, you must be Jessica!" her eyes glow with her brother's mischief as her body springs off the deck. "I've heard a lot about you." Her hand comes to a rest up on Brandon's high shoulder, her lips teasing his face with a smile that turns upward just right.

I feel my cheeks flush; I'm glad of the color discretion that comes with the night time. He must have been talking about me.

Sharron leads us around to the front of the house, where her car waits.

The ride home is fast—I'm home too quickly. Brandon's hands are grasping mine, tight. The front light is on, shining brightly down, lighting the pathway up to Grandpa's steps.

"Meet me tomorrow at lunch," his grip

grows tighter, not letting me leave quite yet.

"Where?"

"Our little house."

His eyes play into mine. Our little house. "I can't be late for class."

"You won't," his hands release.

I know I won't; he won't let me be late. I trust him now, and I think he trusts me.

Dad emerges from the front door and steps into the shine of the light. He stops. Waits on the very top step, arms crossed and lips tight.

My temple shudders at the sight of his lips…I can already hear their sucking noise.

"I have to go…thanks, Sharron." She smiles.

"Wait!" I'm stopped.

Brandon is getting out of the car, too. I'm not sure what to think.

He keeps a step ahead of me, meeting Dad first. Their hands shake. Brandon tells Dad that he's sorry I'm back so late. Dad's nods solemnly; his mouth is visibly angry, but at least his tongue is set away from his teeth. I don't think he quite knows what to make of the situation, but he and Brandon say their goodbyes civilly.

Brandon turns to me and smiles, mischief in his eyes.

"Good night," he says.

My eyes shy down, but a smile escapes. Dad is watching me now. "Good night," I answer.

I am grounded. Grounded until next month. I can only talk to Brandon from home, on the phone. It doesn't really matter, though. My parents don't know that I plan to see him anyway—every day. I will see him every day that I can escape from school at lunch, escape from the sounds and the stares. Escape from the girl who used to be my friend: Abby. I'm glad that she and I are done, because how much can she even care about me anyway? But I'm glad that I am no longer alone now that I've let Brandon in. At least, I think I have…

November: Face the Sound

Mom is waiting out in the lobby hall. Her eyes are fixated on the TV screen, but I'm certain her mind is somewhere else; somewhere far away. Far away behind a wall, behind this wall that separates her from me. This wall separates her, and she can only imagine, for she cannot see me. She cannot hear me. She cannot feel me. She is out there, and I am in here with Lisa—Lisa and her deck of cards.

I tell Lisa I don't want to play. Thank God, I think as she puts the cards away. After a whole hour of listening to her tappity-taps I'd surely react, and I'd surely be locked away. That is not going to happen again. Not today.

Lacking the cards, Lisa's hands begin to

shuffle through some papers on her desk. Then she looks up. Grey eyes peek over the tips of silver glasses. She has silver hair; long, frizzy hair. She has it pulled back loosely above her ears into a thick, wild ponytail, swaying down from a single silver clip. She is like a ball of shimmering tinsel, yet Christmas is still a month away.

Tinsel? My mind is definitely making a mad dash as far away from the present as possible, even farther away than Christmas; even farther away than Mom's mind is from the TV screen she watches.

Mom's mind will only continue to wish she was here where she could see, hear, and feel what is happening in this room. But that won't happen, I remind myself, for she's not allowed in here.

"Any plans for Thanksgiving next week?"

"Huh?"

"Are you having a dinner for Thanksgiving?"

"Oh, yeah. At my Gram's," I respond, although I wish it weren't true.

"Turkey?"

"Yeah."

I need to shift the focus off myself and onto Lisa before the thought of Jeffery's chewing makes me rude. "How about you?" Lisa smiles.

"Yes. My family will be joining me at my house this year. The grandkids are coming all the way from Dallas, Texas!"

I smile back. Really, it's not that I don't like her. It's just that I don't want to be here with her, facing the risk of a conversation that will remind me of sounds I hate (a.k.a. a conversation about Thanksgiving food). Wherever there's talk of food there's the thought of eating, and with the thought of eating comes the thought of Jeffery. Jeffery and his sounds. His mouth-wide-open, smacking sounds.

Smacking and more smacking. Sounds that rage through my brain.

There's no way I can relax here; I have to watch everything that I say and everything that Lisa says. Not only that, but I have to worry that she might start making her own sounds…that double tappity-tap sound. I can't risk my sanity, as much as I still possess. I can't spoil my own plans to get out of here (father from here than just the wandering of my tinsel-tinkered brain—or was that her brain?). Anyway, I guess anything's better than my own hyper-focused, raging brain. And anything's better than Lisa focusing in on it.

She is now pulling her shuffled papers and pencils off the top of her desk. She places the little round coffee table familiarly between the two of us.

"Here," she says, putting paper and pencil in front of me, and then arranging some for herself on top of her desk.

My eyebrows lift in a single question mark.

"Draw, write, doodle. Do whatever you want to do." She turns around to her paper and pencil and begins to do whatever it is she plans to do.

Yes, she is a tinsel brain. Tinkered tinsel-brain. I bite my lip to hold back a laugh. My eyes search the plain, white page, the page

that stares back at me blankly. What to write on it? I suddenly feel as though I'm in the first grade, staring at page that I am supposed to fill in with pictures and misspelled words that might not make sense. My words wouldn't make sense to Lisa, my 'teacher', anyway. She's probably hoping that I will fill in the sheet with my rage—my rage that she will never see or hear. Rage she could never feel, for my rage belongs to me and me alone. All she will ever see in me is a single, blank page; she will never see my anger.

But even so—even though my rage exists only in myself alone— in facing it I have grown less alone. I'm not alone at all, for I let Brandon in. I told him everything: all about the sounds, all about my rage—my uncontrollable, crazed rage that snapped his little stick in two. In dealing with my rage he has now involved himself, too…

*

We're here again, here at "our little house", although, today there is something different about Brandon, something not quite right. I see it in his eyes. Mischievous wolf eyes squint meanly; he does not speak, he only watches me from across the log. He watches my every move, paralyzing me. I cannot speak. What is happening? What did I do?

Brandon's hand lifts slowly, something grasped within it: a little stick. The torture begins. My torture and my rage are ignited in that little stick, in his tapping. Tap-tap-tapping goes on. Brandon taps and stares at me. Tap-tap-tapping...

I can no longer see his eyes; all I can see is his little stick, the stick inside his hand. It's what I see. It's what I hear—that tapping from his hand. My eyes grow thick with rage.

What makes him want to torture me? I have no idea; I don't understand.

Tap-tap-tap... Now I don't even care. Tap-tap-tap... My eyes shoot pain and I swear inwardly...

I curse his stick; I curse his hand; I curse the tapping from his hand. My fists clench tight; my nails dig deep; my sanity is long lost; I feel my inner beast rising.

And then he stops. Just like that. He lifts the stick as raging eyes watch him. He snaps it in half, its final and last tap—just like that.

Just like that? My rage is full force now, and it's me that snaps next. My body bursts up, as his does. My fist meets my head with

its exploding rage. I don't see Brandon move, but like lightning two hands grab my fists and take command.

I feel my voice grate as it lets out a wild shriek, "Brandon, let me go! Let me go! Please!!"

I try to wrench my fists out of his, but only end up strengthening his hold.

"No." His voice is firm yet strangely calm. He won't release me until my anger subsides.

"Do you hate me, Jess?" I don't understand.

"Do you hate me, Jessica?" more

emphatically. "N…no," I guess not.

"Do you hate that little stick?" He grins. Does he really have such evil within him? What is it that you don't like?"

"That stick. That sound! That sound, alright?" The tears feel good as they cleanse my rage. I begin to feel silly; a smile escapes.

Brandon releases my hands and gives them a little rub, pulling me into his embrace.

"Then face it, Jess. Face the sound—fight it. Don't let it win." "I can't!"

"You can. You'll learn. We'll keep trying again." "No!"

"No, not now. But we will, again…"

An hour has almost passed, and no words between Lisa and I have been spoken. I look down at my doodling that has filled the page. Chicken scratch. Two half-formed figures sitting on a log facing each other. Happy, I think. No rage—not on this page. Unless you happen to look close to—what is that?—little broken lines, little sticks, broken in half? Sticks that Lisa will not see. I will never let the rage out of myself;

not here, not in front of her. Never.

She turns her body around, holding up her once blank page.

Her lips smile as she hands it to me. "For you!"

I take the sheet from her hand. It's me. Me, doodling on my once blank page. Why are you a therapist? Is what I want to say. She should be an artist instead. "Can I keep it?"

"Of course!" Lisa pauses, "And how about yours? What did you draw?"

I hand it to her but don't say a word.

"Hmm, nice. Is that you?" She points to the girl-like, chickens cratched figure.

My shoulders shrug. My mouth won't speak. "Can I keep it?" she asks.

"Sure, go ahead," I say. What would I possibly do with it anyway, hang it on the fridge to display?

"Well, that's it for today. See you in another two weeks? We'll make it for the second, a Friday."

"Yeah, ok."

Strangely, I'm out and on my way.

Today is the day that I have come to dread: Thursday the 24th, Thanksgiving. We're arriving at Gramma's. The first meal that I will spend eating with others since months ago, since sending my plate into flight and smashing it to pieces across the room. Both Mom and Dad have already spoken to me. I have no choice, "Thanksgiving is a time for family. For being together, eating together as a family. You will eat with us."

Oh, joy. I know who the "us" is. It's me sitting at the kids' table with my little cousins, Sarah and Gavin, and him—Jeffery. Sitting right next to him. Bumping hands, elbows, feet and legs, all while trying to eat. But all that doesn't matter. It's Jeffery and the sounds that only

he makes: his smacking, his slurping, and his disgusting burping. His mouth will be wide-open, open in my face, smacking and smacking in my ear. A sound that no one else seems to hear, or even care about if they do happen to hear it. But here we are. We're here.

SOUND

Gramma is smiling with her arms wide open.

"Oh, Jeffery! Come here you big, squishy ball of all my lovin'!" Jeffery's body bounds up and is quickly absorbed into her air suctioning hug. She twists him left and right, squeezing him in between her thick arms, enfolding him from sight and then releasing him.

Now her smile centers in on me. Too late; she's already caught me by my hand. "Oh, and my sweet Jessie." She pulls me in and smothers me.

"Hi Gramma..." My voice squeezes out, pushes out from my hug deflated lungs.

I'm released. I breathe. "Come in!" Gramma says.

Everyone's already here (we're always late). But that's just fine with me...except for the fact that it's now time to eat. The family is quickly settling in, surrounding the turkey, gravy, Gramma's 'famous stuffing', mashed potatoes, sweet potatoes, salad, Aunt Sandy's home-made bread, cranberry sauce, and the thick

Italian pole beans sprinkled with olive oil and roasted garlic that Gramma had saved from her little summer garden. Dad's eyes are sparkling, a sight rarely seen, at least by me. He's pulling out his homemade wine for him and Uncle Gary. Everyone will have a glass, even the four of us who sit practically on the floor, wedged together with legs tangled underneath our own miniature table. Even we will get a sip, because "it's Thanksgiving".

Dad's teeth actually grin.

The wine is poured and the food begins to fill our plates. Jeffery tries to take only bread, turkey, and gravy, but Mom serves him more—more than my eyes can bear. My fingers claw down my eyes' only shield: locks of curls. But they spring back up, keeping Jeffery's mouth in sight. I'll just have to focus my eyes off to the other side, or better yet, straight down at my own dish. I feel my stomach turning sick. My temple, for sure, will soon explode. I'm barely making it past Dad's lengthy toast. Everyone's glasses clink, and now Jeffery's teeth are free to sink, mouth open wide, into his food, right next to my exposed right ear.

Smack! It's here. That sound. It's all happening too fast. My finger violently plugs my ear.

Smack, smack! That sound. I can't escape! But now, it's not just in my one ear; it's now echoing everywhere. From all around me. All around the room. Everywhere. Smacking. Circling. Sounding my rage.

If only Brandon were here (…smack)! No, no. Not even Brandon would help me to escape.

"Face it, face the sound," he'd say.

No, no I won't! I can't. Not today!

And so I've lost, again. I can't hold it in. My body bursts in explosive rage, with force untamed. My eyes are burning into Jeffery's. It's him who takes away my sanity.

Jeffery and our cousins grasp their plates tightly. I feel their fear, their fear and guilt. But the guilt is not truly theirs, it is mine. My guilt. Why do I feel this guilt? It mixes with my rage; it tangles with my hate; it points my eyes into their eyes and into their fear, fear that I have created.

I feel more eyes on me, adult eyes joining the eyes of the kids. These eyes can burn me and these eyes do burn me. They burn into me deeply, irate and questioning. They accuse. They point at me. They don't understand—no one understands. They can't; how could they?

My sixth sense detects the sucking of teeth. I need to escape now.

"I have to pee," I lie. I need to escape.

My hands push back my chair. My feet carry me away. I will escape; I cannot let myself hurt Dad. I cannot hurt him. But haven't I hurt him already? Why do I even care anymore?

I'm making my escape. I'm veering my way past the bathroom and heading straight out the back door. I'm outside. Alone. I made it. My feet pace, back and forth, back and forth.

I can't take that sound anymore.

A thick, warm hand grasps my shoulder, turning my body around and stopping my pacing. Gramma. She has followed me out the door. I shudder.

Gramma is calm.

"What's going on with you, my Jessie?" She wipes away my tears— tears that I hadn't realized were there. Tears are a natural, cleansing flow; the flow that washes away my rage and my hate. Tears washes them away and help me to see more clearly. But I can feel it now: the guilt is here, full force. I feel it, clear and heavy. What is happening to me?

"I don't know," I manage a whisper. "I'm sorry, Gramma." My hands shake.

Gramma smiles, but I read sadness in her eyes.

"No, don't be sorry." She pauses. "I understand." Then she lets out a small laugh, "Well, maybe I don't completely...but your Grandpa... now he would."

"Grandpa?"

"Yes, your Grandpa. Never could sit

through a whole meal. Ha! Sweetest thing alive until it was time to eat, but then, watch out! Just ask your dad. He'll tell you." Gramma's thick hand gives my arm an affectionate squeeze.

"Grandpa?" I feel confused. My eyes lift to Gramma's. "I wish he were here right now, Gramma." Sad eyes smile.

"Oh, honey. Me too…me too."

She pulls me in, smushing my face deep into her neck. Her tears are dripping down, trickling down through my curly hair. Together we remember Grandpa. Four eyes lift together; bond together and combine, wet with tears.

Grandpa?

Two hazel stones stare, equally reflecting

the double green glare. Abby is here.

"Well, can't I come in?" Her voice is uncomfortable. I let her in.

"What are you doing here?" my voice speaks coldly as my body turns away.

She follows me to my room and shuts the door.

"Jess, don't you think this has been going on for far too long?" A thinly plucked eyebrow bends up, creating its familiar, sharp 'N'.

"Think what has been going on for too long?" I play dumb. "Us. Or actually, the not us," she raises her other, impatient, plucked brow.

There hasn't been an 'us' for quite some time now. She went her way and I went mine. Now new friends have been occupying her time, and Brandon has been occupying mine. What makes her suddenly, on the spur-of-the-moment, want to be friends again?

"Where's Rochelle?" I make a guess at what must be the one thing going wrong for her.

"Rochelle? What does she have to do with it?"

My silence brings her eyes to grit. Why? Why does she bother to care now? She's the one who left me when I needed our friendship the most. Didn't she?

"Seriously, Jessica," Abby's throat growls.

And really, what makes her think that I need her now? "Really, Abby," my voice sits calm and flat, "No feelings hurt.

We just went our separate ways, right?" I shrug out this lie, the lie that I tell myself; the one lie that I want both of us to believe. But the sudden flush from beneath my cheeks threatens to reveal the truth, and I know that I can't keep it hidden forever.

"That's how you feel? Jess? You don't even care?"

She's exposed my nerve. Twisted and pinched it hard. I don't care?

My voice erupts out of nowhere.

"No, Abby! You're the one who doesn't care! Why did you even come here? Just to rub it all in my face?"

Two sharp eyebrows rise irately, transforming into horns growing up each side of her face.

"To rub what in your face, Jessica? What? The fact that you've flipped out? That you storm in and out of class whenever you feel like it? That you sit around like a zombie with your fingers stuffed in your ears? So what if I hang with Rochelle now? What do you even care?"

Her hazel eyes flare.

Mine glare.

"Abby, just get out of here." I turn my back once more. I don't want her to catch my sudden crash of tears.

And she goes. She is already gone. Her body is slamming out through the house's front door. Our friendship is officially done, before it could even begin to repair. And this time, there's no question to be asked; it is completely my own fault. My fault alone. I pushed her away when she tried to come back, and now she's gone. I doubt that she'll ever try to come back. Not again;. not for me. Not after this. She truly thinks that I am crazy, that I have "flipped." And yes, I have.

So why do I even care?

My body crumbles to my bedroom floor. I should have stopped Abby before she reached my bedroom door. No, probably not—definitely not, for sure. It's better this way. If Abby knew the full truth about my rage, her opinion that I've gone crazy would be confirmed. It's better that I let her go and never let her back in—not until… Well, maybe…if only I could get better. Somehow. I have to find a way to get better. Somehow…

Mom is knocking on my door. "Are you ok?"

"I'm fine," I manage to say. "It's time to go."

Lisa. I forgot all about my appointment today. I can't let her see me this way. "I'll be down in a minute!"

"Hurry up, or we'll be late. We're supposed to be there for 4:00."

SOUND

A chicken scratch drawing of Brandon and I, our feet surrounded by little broken sticks as we sit facing one another on a log, hangs by a single tack on Lisa's wall. She smiles. Her eyes must have followed the path of my own.

"I couldn't resist..." she says, looking up at the picture and then back down at me. "To hang it up, that is. Would you like to tell me about it now that we have more time?"

I'd like to say "not really". But I guess, what's the difference?

I'm stuck here for a whole hour anyway, so, we might as well talk about something. And talking about Brandon would make a much better conversation than what is really filling my head. Abby. Not only that, but I'd much rather use Brandon as my main distraction rather than the other thing, the real reason I'm even here. The reason that Lisa will never find out about, even with it right in front of her face, hanging up by a single tack on her wall: the little sticks snapped in half, all that remained after my sudden attack of rage. Sure, I'll talk about

Brandon.

"It's just me and my friend," I begin. "Oh, what's his name?"

How did she even know that that other chicken scratch was a him?

"Brandon."

"Is he your boyfriend?" she smiles.

"Yeah. I mean, I guess. We hang out a lot." I hope she doesn't want to talk about sex.

Her expression seems to say, hmm, as she studies the chicken scratch some more, "What is that that you are sitting on? Not a couch…right? Does it have legs?"

I stare at the long blob of a log. I always did hate art class, "No, it's a log. Just a log. He made it into a seat. Well, kind of a bench." I never really did know what to call it, other than "just a log."

"A log? Are you outside?" "Sort of. I guess."

I guess it couldn't hurt to tell her about the little house, that is, as long as I don't tell her where the little house happens to be. Right?

Not that she could do anything about it, anyway. I mean, she can't tell my mom; that would break our confidentiality. And really, I'm not doing anything wrong. Well, not that wrong, anyway. I only leave school for lunch, and Brandon always gets me back to class on time. At least, almost always on time.

I feel my forehead scrunching down, forming familiar, crinkling lines: a certain reflection of Mom. I need to stretch it back up, un-wrinkle the stress of my thoughts. Too late. I sense Lisa's eyes inspecting my face.

"So, where are you in the picture?" Surely the question she couldn't resist.

"It's just a little house that Brandon made." Please don't ask me where. Please don't ask me where.

"Hmm," she wonders out loud this time. Did she just notice the sticks?

"Has he built other things as well?"

Out goes my breath of relief, "Um, yes. I think." Her fingers tap twice.

Temple flares. Relief twists and flees,

creating space for the rage forming within me. It seethes inside my twisted brain and out through my eyes, risking proof of my insanity.

Lisa catches this; grey eyes catch mine. My eyes don't see hers, just the tips of her tappity-tap fingers.

I rub my eyes, but I would rather rub my head. Why does this rage happen so fast? Why does her finger-tapping have to be the cause of it?

"Can you please not do that?" The quick snarl slips out of my mouth.

Lisa looks confused. Her fingers tap, once.

"That. Stop that." How are these words escaping?

Lisa's eyes follow mine down to her fingers; the threat of another tap. My fingers find my ears. Water finds my eyes. My feet find the floor in line of obedience with my brain's screaming rage. "Wait," she says. "Stop what?"

"Nothing," I barely can breathe. I force my body back down into the chair. Face the sound. Face the sound.

SOUND

Silence. We wait for the other to speak. To slip. I wait for her to tap, for me to scream. Face the sound. I cannot scream. I have to breath.

I breathe.

My thoughts slowly come back to me. Lisa's eyes watch mine. I am almost calm.

"That tap," I say

I've let her in. I don't know why. Maybe because it's already too late; she's now seen my rage.

"My fingers?" she asks.

"Yes…that tap. That sound. Please stop." She thinks.

"Does it hurt your ears?"

I don't know what to say. It hurts my brain. But that I can't say. "No, it hurts me."

"How does it hurt you?"

"It just…it just makes me angry." "Hmm."

I wish she wouldn't say that. The room grows still. Not a sound.

"How would you describe your anger?" her voice enters back into my head.

"Does it exist in your picture?" Grey eyes look up. Up to the picture tacked onto the wall.

Does she see the sticks? Green eyes grow big.

"The lines. Here…" she found them. Broken, scattered along the penciled-in dirt floor.

Lisa's finger points and follows along, "See how they are so straight and pointed? They almost seem sharp."

My eyebrows raise. I never knew chicken scratch could give all that away.

"And," she goes on, "you're not smiling. Well, you're not frowning, either."

She smiles, and digs in some more. "What story is it that you want your picture to tell?"

One that I would rather keep to myself.

But I don't—not anymore, "It's me and Brandon...the lines— they're little sticks. A stick I broke. I did it because… he tapped it… because he…he wouldn't stop!" Now my voice finally comes to a stop, but not soon enough. Now Lisa really does know. She knows about my rage, my strange, unexplainable rage. She, too, will now think that I am crazy.

"Did you ask him to stop? Like you just asked me?"

"Huh?" I'm caught off-guard. I never really thought about that.

"Uh, no. I guess not."

"Hmm," Lisa repeats that 'thinking sound'. "If you'd like, we could work on ways to help you express your anger more positively. That is," she pauses, "if you'd like."

I don't know what to say or think. I'd never thought to deal with my rage that way, that is, by expressing it. But maybe that's because I can't express it in the moment. Not without letting it thrash out from behind my teeth. No, Lisa's idea won't work.

"No," is all I say. "Ok."

She has nothing more to say? "Ok?" I shoot back.

She smiles, "Whenever you are ready." Her eyes check the time.

It's time to go.

"We meet again in two weeks?" she asks. I shrug 'ok'.

Lisa adds me to her schedule, but stops me from leaving just yet, mumbling something about me having already seen a neurologist. Then she lifts her head and speaks up clearly.

"What would you think of meeting with an ear specialist?" My eyebrows lift.

"You know, maybe there is something we can do. Maybe there's something more to be found—something on the inside. For instance, what if the way the signals run from your ears on up to your brain is not functioning correctly, causing you your feelings of rage?" She actually uses my word, rage. "This could be something that an ear specialist may be familiar with. What do you say?"

"Um…yeah. I guess…ok." My voice is all that answers, for my thoughts are being rapidly left behind. Swirling behind. Lost in the tornado of all this that happens too fast. I thought I was going on this trip alone; I thought I was going to work it out on my own. Figure it out by myself.

Just me. Obviously that did not last for too long…first I let Brandon in, and now Lisa too. But you're still blocking your best friend out, conscience chides.

Well, at least what Lisa says does seem to make some sense. It's fine with me if her idea proves to be true. What if there really is something to be found by an ear doctor? What if there's something he can do to help? I hardly dare to hope.

"Ok then," Lisa smiles. "I'll talk to your Mom and she can have an appointment made."

And that's just what she does.

So now there's a new doctor entering my life. He'll be given the 'right' to examine my crazed and raging brain, even to label me as insane with a nice fat stamp. Or, if Lisa's theory proves to be true,

maybe he'll have the 'raging insanity cure' and zap my rage to goo. Or not. Either way, what I do know is that Mom will not be the one to tell the doctor what's wrong with me. Not this time; not ever again. She does not know the truth, and so her mouth will remain shut. I will ask to see the doctor alone. I will speak for myself, and it will be up to me to tell him what is going on inside my brain. I'll tell him about the pain in my head, sounds turning evil as they paddle up through my ear canals. My words will make their sounds that will spill out from my mouth, and these sounds will enter his ears and paddle up through his ear canals. I can only hope that he'll be able to understand what it is that my sound will say.

Well, I'll find out next Thursday. I'll meet with Dr. Mere. Just me—just me, my sound, and his ears.

December: Safe

Awkwardness breathes thickly, passing back and forth, in and out, Dad's lungs into mine and my lungs into his. This moment we share. Two bodies whose instinct naturally repels now sit together, facing each other. We breathe; we wait. I feel his breath as it combines with my own. I want to move, but my body won't. I sit. He sits. This moment he makes his own: his moment. His moment to show me that he actually cares? Dad. We wait; Dad on his chair, me across from him, and neither wanting to meet the other's eyes or even sneak a glimpse of the other. We wait it out; breathing in, breathing out; breathing the breath of our shared awkwardness. Our silence. Together, this is what we are. What we have become, whenever we are face to face, him and me. The doorbell rings. Brandon and his dad are finally here.

They're here so that I can go. Go with them to their house. Dad said he had to meet Brandon's dad before he'd let me (us) out of his sight. They shake hands, his dad and mine, and we all enter in and sit. A new kind of awkwardness forms: two dads checking each other out and watching each other's kids as well. Now it is Brandon who is sitting across, in Dad's chair, his warm breath mixing deeply with mine. His dad sits next to him, as mine, his arm hairs prickling up along my side as a reminder of his presence, sits next to me. Right next to me. Studying all that Brandon and I do. Reading our secret language that is not meant to be shared. Not with him, at least, or Brandon's father either, for he is watching us too.

Our dads talk. They laugh. They tease.

Then mine finally lets us go. Brandon's dad has passed his test, and Dad trusts me in his care, under his watch. He trusts him to watch over me and his son. They both agree, "no shut doors." That's all my dad seemed to need to know. If he ever found out about our little house, he would surely explode! That is a story that will remain forever and ever untold.

It's strange entering Brandon's house with permission, when we're not supposed to be somewhere else such as school. And people know where we are: at an actual, real house. And people know that we are together. We are together. Strangely, something about Dad knowing makes our relationship feel more official.

Brandon's hand is now leading mine, along with my body, upstairs to his room.

"No shut doors!"

"I know, Dad! Don't worry." We both smile and continue our way. We knew it was coming.

We pass Sharron on our way. She's sitting

on her bed, reading, apparently studying for a college exam with her door cracked open. She doesn't bother to look up. She only waves a hand. To say hi or to shoo us away? I'm not sure which. But it doesn't matter; we're at Brandon's door. He pushes it open and exposes the nonexistent light; a replica of our little house. But unlike that room, this one has a bed. His bed. I feel the sharp chill as it prickles up my neck. I feel my cheeks flush out their heat as they turn red. He pulls me in.

"Should we shut it?" His whisper teases the blush of my cheeks.

My voice doesn't know how to respond; and it doesn't matter, for his lips have found mine, and my body has found his bed with the assistance of his, pushing down on top of me. Heated pressure fills deeply within; inside out; outside in. His breath fills my lungs, seeping down my throat through the passage of his tongue. Did he shut the door? My head can't lift. It's floating, dizzy, squished, sinking deeply down; down into his blanket; down into his bed. His hands wrap my face while my fingers crawl up his back. He's kissing my cheeks, my forehead, my lips. I feel something of his beginning to grow, pushing up between our bodies, underneath his clothes.

"Brandon," I try to speak.

He keeps kissing me; his hands are beginning to search. "Brandon," my voice tries again.

He's smiling now, and kissing me more. His lips eat my words. "Hey, Brandon!" it's Sharron. I couldn't be more relieved, or more embarrassed.

Brandon's head lifts off of mine as his hand snakes out from underneath my shirt. We both sit up.

"Your door was shut," she laughs, and disappears back to her room.

"Oh, thanks!" he calls back after her.

"Whenever you need my help!" she taunts. "Never mind the evil sister-turned-mom."

His eyes squint down into mine. The room is still dark, but his eyes continue on, searching every inch of my face while his fingers play, twirling my locks, tickling the back of my neck. My eyes fade into his; they're asking the single question that my voice will never dare to ask: what gives you the power to make me feel so scared yet so good, all at once? I'm not really sure I'm ready for this, but I know, he is.

"You're shivering," he pulls me in. Although I'm not cold; I'm burning up from somewhere within. One arm wraps tightly around my back, while the other pulls up his blanket. He sits back, kisses my forehead, and wraps me up.

"Brandon," I try again.

His eyes are looking into mine.

I look down. "I don't know if I'm ready for this." Do the sounds of my words even exist?

They do. Brandon lifts my chin back up. "Jess, I would never make you do anything you didn't want to do." His arms take me back in. He holds me close.

I am safe. I am safe. I am safe with him? Brandon, who with a single breath can fill me with fear, then draw me back in again just as quickly. Brandon, who can torment me intentionally, then convince me it's for my own good, who I tried to run from, but ended up running to instead. Brandon. No other has ever filled my head this way. Maybe that's why we're meant to be. He knows me, and yet is not afraid of me, of my rage. Rage that can come and go as quickly as the confusion that pumps inside my head. Maybe I should let him try again to help me with my rage. ...Maybe.

We haven't tried again. Not yet. Not since he snapped his own little stick in half.

So I ask him. He answers with his devious grin. Apparently this is fun for him.

"Come on." He pops up and throws me my coat. "Where are we going?"

"Don't worry, just put it on—it's cold out."

I follow his command and he leads the way. He tells his dad we'll be right back. "Just going for a walk," he says.

His dad lets us go. I don't know why. He trusts him, I guess. Do I?

Brandon takes my hand, and I soon find out if I do. I know exactly where he's bringing me: to our little house. I breathe lightly now, for there I feel safe. But my body shudders knowing what lies ahead. I've put him up to it, though. I told him I'd let him try to make me deal with it, without a fight. Without a fight? I think, for sure, that I've told him my very first lie.

We're here. I don't feel safe—not anymore. What was I thinking? Did I want to instigate my own torture? My legs are stiff. I can't sit. My temple creeps. What was I thinking? What torture will he use? He's studying my face now; the lantern's lit.

He puts out his hand, "Come here, come sit." I barely can make it, but, I sit.

"Are you ready?"

"Y…yes." Another lie, already. "You said eating bothers you?" He's moving too quickly.

"Just Jeffery, I think." Really, I don't know. Since Thanksgiving and before, I have chosen to eat alone. Brandon smiles.

"Let's see."

SOUND

He pops some gum in his mouth and begins to chew, chewing loudly. Chewing slowly. Chewing with his mouth wide open. Wide open with his gum. Chewing and smacking. Smacking, and smacking some more. It's working now; I don't want to do this anymore. This idea was wrong—so wrong. I can't do this anymore. He needs to stop. He needs to stop that sound!

"Just stop," I growl.

He doesn't. He smacks and grins back in my face. Smack. He smacks in my face.

"Stop, Brandon. Stop!!" My feet touch ground; his hand goes out, barring my way. There's no way out...

My body knows better than to attempt a move, but my fingers rebel. Deeply they dig; deep down two holes that lead straight to my personal hell.

Brandon's hands touch mine, but softly. He's no longer chewing, he's just waiting for my calmness to come back.

Come back. I feel myself breathe. I open

my eyes to find his, just waiting for me.

"Ok?" He smiles. This time, he's sweet.

"Ok," I whisper.

I can finally breathe.

I tell him that I don't ever want to try to face it again. Never again. He asks me if I'm sure…of course I don't answer. His eyes

sweep down into mine, sweeping away every stray speck of fight left in me. If only his eyes could seep down into my brain, inside my rage, and sweep it, too, cleanly away. If only…

But he can't. No one can—not me, not him. Not anyone. Every doctor that I have ever seen has read me wrong, telling me I'm something that I am not. Treating me for things that are not a part of me, or for things that only form a part of me. For all that the doctors have tried to treat me for comes from a different cause, something that even they don't understand. No one does. Not me, not them. There is no cure. There is no hope. I am hopelessly crazy. There, my story's told.

But…is it? Is that really all there is? The

answer is—nothing? There's nothing a single person can do? I am damned to live the rest of my life this way, one big raging mess out on my own? It can't be. That can't be all there is. There has to be more; there has to be an answer, a way to fix my rage and wash it away. To make me sane again. Was I ever sane? I'm sure there was a time when I was. Anyway, in a few days I will meet Dr. Mere, the ear doctor. And once again, I will not allow Mom's words to be heard, just mine. Just mine and the doctor's. I only hope that he can find a way to help me, to give me my cure. To take away my rage.

Please, just take it away.

December: Dr. Mere

Firecrackers. They crackle when they're lit. Sizzling fire, a tapping fit. Underneath my chewed nails the sparks ignite; firecrackers erupt, igniting my fight. My fight that was hers, but which she's spread; it sizzles out hot through her tapping nails. She didn't like my words; I don't like her sound. Mine were short; but hers, prolonged. I told her no, "No, don't come in," and that is what caused her tapping to begin. When firecrackers begin, they seem never to stop. Crackling, tapping, my brain will soon pop.

"Jessica?"

I jump to my feet. I am saved. I give the

offender a glare and a wave. I see her mouth open, but she is too late; I am following the nurse. I have escaped.

Unfortunately, my brain has not escaped. I rub my temple. The tingling won't stop. Please, please, why won't it just stop?

The nurse is giving me a funny look…tapping. I wish that the sound would come unstuck; it's echoing, repeating, torturing, tapping, crackling, stuck in my head.

"Is everything ok, Jessica?" The nurse's face is also stuck; she looks at me with a funny expression. She must wonder what's up.

"Yes. Is there a bathroom I can use?" My answer, to me, sounds confused. The nurse points my way, my way to escape.

I shut the door quickly and lock it tight; my fist finds my temple…the tingling…the repeating, it must come to a stop… My fist pounds my head …Just let it stop.

It stops. My face is red, but I don't care. I splash cold water up over my temples and into my ear. My temple pounds, but the sound is gone. I choose pain freely, for it kills the sound.

I open the door to find the nurse is waiting. Waiting right there.

Did she hear the pounding of my fist? Not a word escapes her lips.

She leads me into Dr. Mere's examination room—me and my red face. The water didn't work. Surely, this nurse thinks that I'm crazy.

I'm so glad when she finally leaves. Now I just wait, wait for Dr. Mere. I hope that Lisa was right. I hope that he can help, that maybe he'll know what I am talking about when I tell him about my pain… although I don't think that he will. I don't think it's actually my ears. It has to be something up inside my brain, or somewhere along the way. The sounds that enter in do so just like regular sounds do, right? But then there must be something going wrong after that, because the sounds grow. They change. They become their own, and drive me insane. No, I already am insane, I think. But, that's not the point. The point is, does the doctor know about more than what lies within just one's ears? Will he be able to help me with what his eyes can't see, with what lies past my eardrums, deep inside my brain? I guess all I can do is sit here and wait...

Dr. Mere finally knocks on the door. He walks in, smiling, shaking my hand. He is nice. My lips almost form a smile of their own, but my temple still hurts. It's pounding out its unforgiving pain. It will not let me forget, and neither will I.

Dr. Mere begins by asking me a few questions: what brings me here, what type of sounds, where is the pain, does my anger last long, how long has this been going on, have my symptoms worsened over time? Then, he checks inside each ear, down my throat, and up my nose. He lets me know that "everything looks great." My eardrums look perfectly healthy, he says. Then he tells me to wait; a nurse will come back in soon and take me into another room, where I'll have a hearing test done. I doubt they'll find anything wrong. I already know that I can hear perfectly well.

Too well. Would he mind, instead, to help me to remove my hearing? That I could live without. Without a sound to hear, my rage would have no way in. It would simply disappear. Vanish. Be gone! I wish he could take away all the sound…

The hearing test tells the truth, just like I thought it would: nothing's wrong. Not in my ears. Dr. Mere says there's not a lot that he can do, but that there's one more test that might be of use. An ABR, that is, an "Auditory Brainstem Response Test". This test will tell if sound is taking the right path into: from my ears, through my nerves, and on into my brain.

I'm not so sure that Dr. Mere's words have just been translated correctly within my mind. Did he just say that he wants to check the passages that go from my ears and into my brain?

"Yes!" The word has never left my mouth so quickly. Dr. Mere smiles and says he'll schedule me in.

I love this doctor. My God, I love him!

December: Anything or Nothing

Monday. All that starts with 'm' is evil: Monday, Mom, meeting, mad. Mad Mom at the Monday meeting, that is. We're here, back at school, meeting once again with my guidance counselor, Mrs. Peters. No one is happy. I have not made up any schoolwork. My head remains on my desk day to day, class to class. My grades have gone down under, further than they were before: from D's to F's. I am now officially failing almost every single class.

"Why haven't you gone to see Mr.

Rolland if you're upset?" Mom is demanding. Her left eye twitches in irritation.

I know better than to give her an answer. It would only cause her eye to twitch some more.

"Jessica, there still is a ways to go before reaching the half way point for this school year," says Mrs. Peters. "It is very possible for you to bring your grades back up. But it's also up to you to make it happen. You are the one that has to put in the extra effort." She waits for my response, a response that has no intention of ever surfacing. A response that she would most likely ignore, anyway.

Finally, she proceeds, "Your grades are your responsibility, Jessica. It's all up to you." Her hands flip up. Her curse to the sky?

Another twitch.

My green eyes drop to the floor.

I feel two sets of eyes staring intently into those of the other, passing by right over my head. I'm sure Mom's left eye is giving yet another one of its sporadic twitches. I'm glad I can't see it. Instead, my eyes are stuck to the floor; glued deep down, stuck in my own sticky mess. A mess that there is really no way out of—a mess that I have not created, at least not intentionally.

But the mess is there. Really, it is everywhere. From class to class my mess exists. It forms into existence with each and every offending sound that travels up into my brain.

Old sounds, new sounds, drive-me-insane sounds; all of the school sounds that create my rage. The sound of Mr. Owens' raspy voice, finger tapping, pens and heels with their click, click, clicking, the gum induced, mouth-wide-open, smacking, and now even the constant, never-ending, disgusting sniffling. Doesn't anyone know how to blow their nose? All I can do is sit in the back corner of each and every class with my head on my desk and fingers stuffed deeply into my two tormented ears. My ears screech their pain day after day, begging for me to stop as the sharp nails enter in, stuff, and twist. Twist away my rage. I would rather my ears die an agonizing death than to let my rage take control.

"Jessica, are you willing to even try to do your work?" It's Mom, and she's desperate.

Shoulders shrug. Eyes are still stuck; mouth shut.

"What other options do we have?" Mom's pitch is high, too high, making my right temple to cringe. A single finger tangles tightly around and around, yanking out strands of my hair, locks that have failed to guard my sanity from all the sounds that enter in.

"Well..." Mrs. Peters stops to think. "Well, we could work on an IEP for Jessica."

Aren't IEPs for special needs kids? Well, I guess these days I'm fitting that role just about right.

"An IEP? What's that?" Mom is lost.

"An IEP is an Individual Education Plan. They are used when a student cannot...well, when the regular classroom setting is just not working out. Which seems maybe to be the case with Jessica."

My eyes pluck up, finally unstuck from their sticky mess. They look directly at Mrs. Peters. I'd rather not look to see if Mom's eye is making another twitch, which it is surely doing.

Strangely, for once Mom seems to be at a loss for words.

And what's even more strange is that my own words seem to exit straight out of my mouth unexpectedly.

"There's nothing you can do to help."

The words were rash, but they spoke the truth. Really, what could they possibly do? Put the whole school on mute? Now that's something I'd like to see them try to do.

Mrs. Peters apparently does not like my response, or maybe it's the tone of my voice—probably both.

"Maybe you need to give us a chance, Jessica."

This time I keep my response to myself. And, seemingly, we have all been put on mute. Not even our bodies seem to dare attempt a move. We sit motionless, all except the twitch of Mom's eye, and my eyes that have happened to catch the motion as they dared to drift.

"Well, what can you do?" It's Mom. "Well, we could set her up with tutors." "Tutors?"

And there they go. Two people talking on and on about me as if I had somehow, mysteriously, disappeared from the room. Well, I am here. Right here. I have not left, and my ears do hear—very well, at that.

They're coming up with a plan, their plan for me. But what they don't know is that this time I will intervene, if or when there comes a need.

But, I don't intervene. I actually might like their plan for me, meeting with tutors outside of class. Not having to set foot inside a single room. Yes, I could actually like this plan...yes, I do. I wouldn't even have to set foot in the school! And, not only that, but did they actually just think to ask me? Am I stuck in some kind of twisted dream? They asked me where I would want to meet? I have been given my own choice? Without a fight? This is crazy! This is a plan that I might not fight.

So today I get to go home. Home before I have even set foot in a single class. Mrs. Peters says it will probably be a few days before they can have the tutors set up, most likely a different tutor for each subject. We'll meet at the public library, away from the school. Far away from the school. My dream has come true, at last.

Yes, but what about my time with Brandon at our little house?

Well, maybe it doesn't really matter. We have both come to agree that soon it will be too cold for us to meet. And, as long as I can stay un-grounded, we can still see each other every day after my time at the library, at his house or mine. And on weekends we can see each other all day long. So really, I have nothing to lose.

Or do I? With the end of my school life, does all hope of ever rekindling my friendship with Abby end too? It already seems pretty hopeless. The last time we even spoke was at my house, when she came there to try to talk and I told her to just get out. Why do these thoughts even bother to come back? Why do they continue to keep filling my head? She hates me. To Abby, I'm already dead. Dead crazy. But still, I can't help but wish for her to come back, for us to rebuild our friendship—our trust. I miss Abby. She and I had always been best friends. Now I'll probably never see her again, and she probably won't even know that I'm gone. And if she does, will she even care? No, her days of caring have long been over.

Yet can't all of this change? Tomorrow I will meet with Dr. Mere again. I'll have the ABR done and see if he can find anything wrong. But even if he does find something, even if he can fix it, is it already too to save face? If he can take away my insanity, will anyone even notice the change? I'm the crazy girl who sits in the back of the class, never talking to anyone, just sitting head down, ears stuffed; the girl who has been known to randomly jump up with a red face and flooding tears, when nothing was even said. Who would even want to be my friend? Not Abby. Not anyone.

The only one who will even come near me is Brandon, maybe because he doesn't see me in class. He's a year ahead, and really, does he even make it to class at all? He spends more time in detention than he does anywhere else. But still, he knows me. He knows every inch of my rage. He knows how to inflict it and then wait for it to go away. He also knows that it will not go away, that it will come back, but even that doesn't scare him away. He has made me his own personal game, a game for him to be the first to win. He wants to make my rage go away and never come back again. If only there was a way to cheat, I'd let him win. If only it was an actual game, instead of the reality of my own personal, craze-inflicted brain.

I'm lying here, eyes popped open, lying back rigidly on the reclining, paper covered chair. Sticky things with wires attached are glued all over my head. My eyes are stare skittishly into the eyes of a mad scientist. He laughs and says, "This won't take long now. You won't feel a thing." He must be getting ready to zap my brain.

Of course, he doesn't. And no, I don't feel a thing. I'm just lying here listening to funky sounds and clicking, while a machine reads the nerves passing their waves to my brain. Can they even be read through all the glue? Are the sounds even taking the right route to my brain? Supposedly, the wires roping along to the machine will soon tell. I can't relax. I need to know. And, not only that, but I don't know what's worse: having these sticky things stuck all over my head, or the clicks being force fed through my ears. Can those squiggly lines coming out from that machine really interpret my rage? Really, what will they even say?

Finally, the test is done. The mad scientist turned doctor shows me back to the waiting room, where I wait. Me and Mom. Dr. Mere will look over the results, and then I'll be called back in.

Mom is restless. I know that she wants to come in with me. I guess it wouldn't hurt for her to be included this time, I mean, there's nothing that she could possibly say now that would change anything. And if something is actually wrong, it would be easier for her to hear it from the doctor than from me. Really, how would I even be able to explain it?

So Mom comes in with me, and we find that there's nothing to be explained. There's nothing wrong (so the doctor says). I want to scream. I wish now that Mom hadn't come in. I want to demand that the doctor tell me what's wrong. Now. Something—anything.

"What about the pain?" My desperation has flipped its lid. Because what I really want to ask is about my rage.

The doctor's eyebrows lift. He looks at Mom. I want her out.

"If there's nothing wrong then how do you explain what's been going on?" More words spurting out, like projectile vomit spewing out from my mouth.

"Jessica, there really isn't much that I can do. I'm sorry. Please know that I do believe you when you say that you're experiencing something."

I feel myself losing control. The tears are flooding down my cheeks.

"Your hearing is excellent, and your ear drums are perfectly healthy. The ABR shows that the sound is traveling correctly from your ears to your brain. It could just be that you have overly sensitive hearing. In some people, certain sounds can actually seem as though they are being amplified, which has been known, at times, to cause pain."

But it's not just pain, it's rage. Rage that causes pain, which is triggered from just the thought of certain sounds. Does amplified

hearing do this as well? I think not. Why did I let Mom come in with me? Now my words must come to a stop once again. I am silenced. I silence myself. I choose to keep

Mom out. My body stands up. My feet take me out. Mom will hear no more of what I wish I could say, what I would say if only she weren't right here. Why did I let her in?

I go to the car; I just want to go home. To think I actually thought this doctor could help, that maybe he'd have the answer to my rage. No. Nothing, just 'amplified hearing'. Sure, I hear alright, but that's not what it is. I know it's not. It's not about my hearing, it's about how my brain interprets the sounds. It's about how it all turns, so suddenly, into rage.

A long time seems to have passed before Mom finally comes out of the building. She's holding a paper in her hand, folding it, and putting it away in her purse. A little secret of her own? She unlocks the car doors without saying a thing, and gets in. We ride home quietly, in silence, each holding our own secrets within. Neither of us has a single word to share with the other. Nothing. Not a thing.

December: Death

There is still no snow. Even with the numbing air that fills my lungs and drifts back out and away for miles around, snow still does not come. Where is the peaceful white blanket, the blanket that wraps and covers every year over the rolling hills, across the fields, and deep into the lakes and streams, hiding everything from the eyes that had predicted and then witnessed the unstoppable death of the earth? The blanket does not exist. The trees' limbs, their trunks, their roots that pop up from their layers of protection in the frozen dirt, the brown grass, and the water that trickles, too cold to touch, all are exposed.

SOUND

There is no cover. There is no blanket of snow.

I am the death of the earth that holds no snow. I, too, have no cover. Many have predicted my certain death and then watched as my sanity was laid to rest. And here I lie, naked, unshielded, with no blanket to cover me up. The air is cold, yet that is not enough. It manages to numb the eyes that look at me, but it is not enough to hide me completely; it only makes it more difficult to see me. It conceals me like the grey cloud that looms over our heads, blocking out the warmth of the sun, showing us that winter has just begun but never producing a snowflake. Not a flake of snow will fall. There's not a thing to cover me up…

Lisa looks concerned as we sit face to face. My eyes have drifted into her two grey cloud-eyes that look back from above, wishing for them to cover me up and blanket me with snow. They won't; they'd rather I stay exposed. They linger there, just above where they can plainly see the death of my sanity. They decide, echoing the decision of the real December clouds, that they too will not cover me. They tell me that I need, instead, to be set free, to rise back up from my death. They tell me I need to try again. This is crazy; not a word has been spoken and yet my eyes are dripping wet.

Lisa hands me a tissue, but still does not speak. And so my words begin. They tell her about Dr. Mere. They tell her about nothing. The nothing. The nothing that he found. It was all a waste of time. I want to tell her my desire to die…but I don't. For if I decide that the time has come to die, I will not be stopped…

There's not much that Lisa can do. She keeps me for an hour and then lets me go, scheduling me in for my next appointment and letting me know that I can call her any time before we meet again. She seems uneasy as she lets me go. I assure her that I'll be fine, but she knows it's all a lie; her two grey eyes tell me so. December: Christmas Eve

SOUND

It's Christmas Eve, and I have not yet put myself to death. The thought does keep coming back, though, day after day as I fight my rage, rage that comes from 'nothing', so it's been said.

Tonight, Brandon will spend time with his family, and I'll spend time with my own. Visions of Thanksgiving are still fresh in my head as we arrive at Gramma's once again. She has baked a ham: smothered it, browned it, and covered it with her pineapple glaze. I almost don't mind that I am being forced to stay. Almost. I really don't want to create another holiday scene. Dad has already threatened me in the hope that I won't. But surely, by the end of the night, I'll be told that I'll be spending my entire Christmas vacation grounded at home. Alone, locked in my cell. I'll be allowed my one phone call, right? Is there any chance of freedom by bail? Yeah, right.

Dinner isn't quite ready, so Mom tells me to go help Gramma set out the plates. Gramma smiles as I step into the dining room with my hands open, receiving, unsteadily, her pile of leaning plates—special holiday china that I dare not drop. I grip them tightly. Gramma follows me out of the china closet, holding her own pile tightly as well. Not that what she holds could actually break, for she holds silverware and cloth napkins delicately trimmed with white lace. She sewed them when she was just a little girl.

She watches me as I carefully align each plate in its place. She follows me with her napkins and silverware, setting them down one by one into their own perfect places. I feel her eyes as they watch me, but she's not so much watching what my hands are putting down; she's watching every expression of my face, every expression that my face loves to tell against my will. I'd rather she doesn't see what I'm trying to keep in: anticipation of the agony I'll feel when the sounds of eating begin. But she sees; I can feel that she does.

The table is now set, but Gramma says she still has one more thing for me to do. She leads me away from the family and into the privacy of her bedroom.

"Here," she says, holding out something small that I can't yet see.

I reach out my hand and take it into my hands: two small pieces of purple foam.

"What are they?" I can't help the look of confusion that's overcome my face.

She laughs.

"Ear plugs." Her face can't help but grin.

"Ear plugs?"

"Here, let me help you put them in."

Gramma takes the ear plugs from my hand and tells me to watch. She twists one into a funny shape, then pushes back my locks and, shoves it right into my ear, right there where my fingers have jabbed time and time again. Right to that exact place, where my fingers have twisted and clawed in the hope that my ears will die a sudden death. And then, in goes the other one. My ears are now plugged. Shut.

"How's that?" I can hardly make out

Gramma's voice, and the earplugs don't even hurt. They don't give the pain that my fingernails give. They definitely work better than my fingers ever have.

A smile escapes my lips as tears slip out.

"No, we'll have none of that," Gramma says as she wipes them away. "Consider it a gift from your Grandpa, from up above."

Through the earplugs her voice seems so far away. So quiet. Her gift, a gift of near silence, brings me peace. I am so glad that I am here with her. I am so glad that she is who she is.

We both smile. And Grandpa. I had forgotten what Gramma had said, how he couldn't make it through a single meal, "sweetest thing alive until it was time to eat." Was he really like me? Am I really like him?

"Did he wear earplugs, too, Gramma?"

A deep, bubbling laugh pours out from her mouth; I watch it form, boil up from her belly, and roll out from her mouth, "Oh, Honey, only when he was around me. Only when we would eat. He was too embarrassed to wear them outside of the house. And anyway," her cheeks plump up with her simmering grin, "he would just say that he couldn't stand all of my 'horrible crunching', even when my mouth was shut so tightly!"

We stand looking at each other, smiling into each other's eyes. I imagine Gramma's eyes turning into little black polka-dots, playing hide-and-seek with mine that look back into hers. Gramma's eyes shine with Grandpa's love and the understanding that only he had. If only he was here.

I make it through dinner for the first time in months. Or has it been a year? Gramma actually sits at the kids' table, directly across from me, so our eyes can meet. So mine can scream all their tortured

pain and rage into hers. She told me to; she said it was ok. She wanted me to be able to stay, and so I did with the help of her eyes and of my new savior, the little purple earplugs.

Of course, the earplugs don't shut out

every sound. But with Gramma's continuous talking, and laughing, and her eyes to calm me, Jeffery's smacking is almost pushed away. I mean, I've just made it through an actual dinner today! And the only reminiscence of Jeffery's smacking is just a speck of tingling that has remained in my head. My hand brushes it away; it leaves slowly, but it does go away.

And so I've made it through dinner, and now we're walking through the tall carved doors of Gramma's church. We're here with her for the Christmas Eve service where all they do is sing hymns and pray. Gramma says it's her favorite night. Her arm takes mine in hers as she leads us down the aisle two by two. I imagine we're entering Noah's Ark, or wandering our way up to Heaven. Everyone is quiet, eyes closed, all praying. Each man, woman, and child sits with heads down and hands closed. They are silent. We sit in our pew. Even Jeffery is quiet. This must be Heaven. This must be what it is like when one is with God: peaceful, soundless, quiet; no rage. I put my head down, close my eyes and feel my hands come together. I pray. I thank God for this night. I thank Him for Gramma. I tell Him to please give Grandpa a kiss up there in Heaven; a silent kiss. For now I know, that Grandpa, too, would only want a quiet one. Not a single sound echoes through the church. I wonder if this is what it's really like up there in Heaven. If it is, then that is where I want to be. It's where I wish I was right now—with Grandpa.

December: New Year's Eve

Brandon's dad is talking with mine out on Brandon's front step.

It's 9:00 now, and Dad wants me home "by 1:30am—no later." Brandon is making a plan with his dad: his dad will drive me home. My Dad just drove away. He let me stay! Brandon's family is having a New Year's Eve party with all of their friends: Brandon's, Sharron's, and even a few of their dad's. Of course, story of my life, I'm the last one here. But who cares? Dad actually let me stay!

The music is playing a random mix that must be a strange attempt at a family compromise; Brandon's dad's classic rock is popping in and out, mixing in-between with Sharron's hip hop. The tone bounces back and forth; the house has become stuck in a continuous shake. Everyone's dancing, talking, laughing, and eating. And strangely, the eating I actually don't think I even mind. I can't hear a thing— nothing, not even the sounds in front of my own face. And anyway, it's not like I actually have to look. Whenever I see something pop in someone's mouth, my eyes can just take off quickly in the other direction.

Brandon has grasped me by my hand and is now leading me through the hot, thickly packed, moving-and-thumping group of Sharron's dancing friends. Their bodies move rapidly with the beat; their feet have become the beat. They pound up and down heavily on the floor. Rapidly. Loudly. I feel them as they pound. The beat pounds; their feet pound. I feel their vibrations, jumping, playing hopscotch up my body from my feet into my heart. My heart fights back; its beating is off.

I watch Brandon's mouth. It hasn't

stopped moving, but his words don't reach my ears. They can't. Only the beat can reach there. Maybe he's giving introductions to everyone that we pass. His lips grin as he speaks; they tease my face. His eyes squint; his mischief escapes, on the rise. The night, the music, has brought him to life. I try to push away my thoughts. I try to ignore the repetitive pounding, the thumpity-thumping, the beating that's overtaking my heart's own rhythm. I know Brandon's teasing will pass. And surely I can overcome my heart's wild beating. I will make me make it through this night. A little thumping can't really stop my heart, right?

We've finally made it to the kitchen, where the noise is at least a little bit quieter. I can now hear the sound of Brandon's voice. And, it's here where we are met with the familiar faces: De'Sean, Kristen, Genevieve, and Eric; the faces of Brandon's friends. They're sitting around the table waiting for him to bring me in. I know them all, well just about as much as they know me. This is the first time that he has brought us together. It's not that we don't like each other, it's just that we've never actually hung out. They're all a little bit older, from a different crowd. A crowd that Abby and I would have never even considered hanging out with. As if we were too good for them? My cheeks grow red.

"Hey, Jess!" It's Kristen. She pulls out the chair next to her.

My eyes meet Brandon's; his encourage me to sit with her. "Go sit—us boys are going out to play." His grin leaks out more of his mischief, pouring it over his friends. Brandon releases my hand as he kisses the top of my head. Three boys laugh. He leads them away.

I sit, nervous. "Where are they going?"

Genevieve laughs, "Oh, don't worry about them." Her eyes meet Kristen's as their mouths take form, hinting at their silent talk. It's too soon, of course, for me to share their trust, their secrets. But hopefully I will soon.

Brandon's dad is walking in, holding the hand of his friend Clarisse. She smiles. "Where are the boys?" Her voice is loud, as the music still pounds heavily into the kitchen.

"They're outside. I think Eric wanted a smoke." Kristen's tongue is fast. Just as fast as Genevieve's hand that raps her on the leg.

"Oh," says Brandon's dad. He once made it clear to me how he feels about "kids" smoking. He said that he's really glad that I don't.

The adults turn their backs as they fill a bucket with ice. Kristen's hand covers her mouth in an attempt to stop a laugh. Genevieve's eyes are big; they swallow up Kristen's as her eyebrows rise and disappear into the thickness of her dirty blonde hair. I wonder why she acts so mean? But Kristen doesn't seem to care. I guess that's just the way their friendship is, kind of like Abby and me...at least, kind of like what we used to be. Abby always had to be in control. I realize now that I don't miss our friendship at all. Abby would never have sat here, not with these people. She thinks they're all no good, that all they do is skip school and waste their lives away getting drunk and high. But I've been with Brandon for about two months and I haven't touched a thing, not once. Neither has he. Well, at least not in front of me, but I think he does do it with his friends. These friends.

My stomach flips in a sudden turn. Is that why Genevieve's hand rapped Kristen so hard on the leg? What are they doing out there? Is that what the mischief was that I had caught escaping Brandon's eyes, the mischief escaping that grin? Is that how he and his friends 'play'? I wish I could stop these thoughts from entering my head. I wish I could push them away.

Brandon and his friends finally come back in. I can't help but check their eyes—no, nothing. Open and clear; no squinting, no red. I feel the relief pour out from my breath as Brandon's body finds its way to the back of mine. His hands wrap loosely around the front of my neck. His chin rests on the top of my head.

"You girls having fun?"

Kristen and Genevieve's eyes meet his over my head. "Wouldn't you like to know, Brandon." Genevieve's blue eyes flirt openly with his, then glimpse slyly down into mine.

I imagine Brandon's mouth forming its grin. I imagine his eyes flirting back into hers. But of course I can't see, for his chin still rests on the top of my head. His arms give me a gentle squeeze. I feel the heat of his breath as it drafts down the back of my neck. It seeps, hot and wet, into my skin as he kisses me softly underneath my hair, on the back of my neck. I shiver. I relax. Brandon doesn't give in to Genevieve's playful taunt. He is here with me and only me. She will not get his attention.

The night goes on: talking, laughing, my eyes swerving whenever I see someone eating, and then coming back when they're done. The tingling comes and goes, but I try not to rub my head. Brandon catches me once and takes my hands in his. He places them on his cheeks, making my eyes connect with his. I can hear his words that aren't audible but pass through his eyes, into mine. Face the sound… face the sound. If only I really could.

I think I do like Brandon's friends, and they seem to like me. I don't think I'll ever get too close to Genevieve, though. No, she's too much like Abby. Does that make Kristen the same as me? I find myself watching her throughout the night in an attempt to find out. But no, I don't think so. No, she's not really like me—she's definitely too sweet. Not a single hint of the rage that comes and goes inside of me.

The time has gone by quickly. It's already 11:00, and the music is suddenly being turned down low. Too low, causing my brain's torment. I hear Sharron telling her friends something about the neighbors. I can't make out all that she says, but what I do know is that it's time for me to get out of this kitchen, and I need to get out now. But how?

Brandon and De'Sean are in the midst of a conversation, while Eric hangs close by us. Well, by Genevieve. She's made her way up onto his lap and they're sharing a non-alcohol Shirley Temple. But that's not what's bothering me; no, it's the sound she's making— the sound that she has been making. Now that the music's been turned down low, the sound has suddenly been amplified. Although I know that, in reality, it's just a discreet little slurping sound, it rages through my ears. My eyes glare at the straw that is constantly slurped by Genevieve. I'm scared that her eyes will take notice of mine, but mine won't let go their grip. They're clutching tightly, they're swearing fiercely; my body is leaping up. I'm out of here.

I manage a quick mumble as I leave, something about being right back. I don't know if they heard me, but I know I won't be back. My body passes Brandon's, moving real quickly. There's no way that he's going to catch me; my rage has flicked my switch. But my body doesn't take me far, just out of the kitchen. It's bringing me up the stairs, to the darkness of Brandon's room. I don't care if he follows me, really, but I'd rather just be alone so

I can disappear from every sound and vanishing from this world.

Of course, he has followed. He stands in the doorway, eyes are searching for me but unable to find me in the dark. He walks in and turns on his light. He looks at me as I cry and shuts the door tight.

Suddenly I'm in his arms, but I want to push him away. Why is he with me? I'm just a crazy ball of rage. Tonight should be the night that I finally disappear, go away from all of this forever. I do not belong here. Not in this world. Not in this life. Not in this house. Not in his arms...not with him. Not with anyone.

There's something wrong with me, and there's just no way to fix it. Tonight is the night that I will fix it, since nothing else can. I will bring it to its end. I cannot kill my rage, so I will kill myself instead.

I push him away. "Brandon, I need to go home."

He looks confused as he asks me what is wrong. I don't have an answer for him. My eyes look down. Tears fall; I watch them hit the ground.

"No."

My eyes lift a little. "Not until you talk."

They're down again. There's nothing for me to tell him… I study the drop of a tear as it crashes to the floor.

"Is it the sound?" he asks.

My head rebels, nodding a little yes. Why is there always a part of me that loves to tattle?

"Come here." Brandon tries to pull me back in close to him. My body fights him, tense, but slowly lets him win.

And now he wins another victory, for words are escaping my mouth. They let him know my plan. My plan that's been foiled now that I've let him in.

"Jess, you're not leaving. I won't let you go. You're staying here with me. I'll never let you go do that." His arms hold me so close to him. My body has stopped resisting; I never want to go from him.

What had made me want to leave him? In death I'd be alone. Now, I know, I would hate to be alone.

My lips brush soft curls, the silk upon his chest. My hands are wrapping slowly, searching the warmth around his neck. Strong hands make their way up, tickling my back softly. Brandon lets one hand slide down over my breast, to my waist. My body tingles hotly as his fingers undo my pants. I know I should stop him, but my words no longer exist. Not one comes out from within me, my lips just meet his in a kiss. His tongue finds mine; fingers prowl, deep and wet. I feel his body growing, persuading mine to dissolve. I really should stop him, but, I don't want to now…

Suddenly he stops. His hands slip out from underneath my clothes. They wrap around my face. His eyes look at me, moist and warm.

"I really like you, Jessica." Then why'd you pull away?

"I don't want to hurt you." Then take me back again.

He pulls me back in, but his hands do not search. He holds me closely. He smoothes down the back of my shirt.

"It's ok," I tell him.

He kisses the top of my head, "No…no, it's not. I can't hurt you like this."

"Like what?"

"Like this. I mean, you were just wishing you were dead! You're not ready, Jess. I won't take advantage of you like this."

"You're not."

"No, I am…You know I want you, Jess…God, I want you…but I will wait."

I feel his warmth. It seeps out from his eyes and into mine; it makes me understand. He is right. I'm not ready. I'm so glad I am with him…

Soon it's 11:55, and we're all downstairs. Brandon's dad has the TV turned on loudly. They're counting down the minutes in New York City. We're counting down here, too. Brandon's dad quickly pours out glass after glass of champagne. We're all stuffed in, elbow to elbow, in the little living room where we'll all make a toast. We'll clink our glasses together; we'll welcome the New Year in. And me—wanting to die—I'll toss it to the moon. 2012 is almost here, and strangely I am not gone. I am still alive and breathing, even with all the sound.

Brandon's arm is wrapped around me, his other arm around Sharron. She's smiling and talking to me, though I don't know about what. It doesn't really matter anyway. I just smile back at her and lift my glass. The ball is dropping…2012, at last!

January 2012

I just met with Ms. Mackie. I saw her twice last month, the Monday and Wednesday before Christmas break. She's one of my new tutors; she teaches me English and Social Studies. She's ok, I think.

Mr. Miller is, too. I study with him every Tuesday and Thursday for Science and Math, two hours for each class. So I only have 16 hours of school each week. What's that—half the time of a regular school week? I guess I can't complain too much. At least, not yet. I've scrambled up some half-truths about my ears being "out of whack". I told both of my tutors that I have sensitive hearing and certain sounds really hurt me. I mean, it's true, right? Well kind of, anyway. Ms.

Mackie asked if that's why I left school. I told her it was. I gave them each a list of sounds that "hurt my ears the worst". They each told me, in their own way, that it's no problem. They said I just have to let them know if they're doing something that causes me pain. But so far there's been no pain. Not yet, anyway.

It really hasn't seemed so strange, the past few weeks, being out of school. But now it's starting to sink in—hard. It's not that I like school, or even that I'm starting to miss it. No, that will never happen, at least I can't imagine it. It's done—my days there are officially over.

I will never have to step foot into that cursed building again, ever. But then why did I develop this sudden lump of a feeling? The feeling has settled deep down in my gut—a heavy, empty hole of a feeling, a something's-gone-wrong, something-is-missing kind of feeling. Does that mean that I actually do miss school? How would that even make sense? How could I actually miss the forceful submersion into that world of torture or the pain that evolves from within each and every classroom, from every hall? How could I miss all the sniffling, clicking, and the smacking of gum? Really? What am I thinking?! It's not possible that I could actually miss the source of all the sounds of my Hell.

Now I'm with Lisa, on a Monday, which is unusual. I don't know why we're meeting on a Monday; I think the holidays just mixed us up for a while. It's the first time I've seen her since I wanted to die. She looks relieved. She says that I look a lot better; she smiles and asks me how I'm doing.

I tell her I'm doing alright.

"Nothing new, really," I lie. There's no point in telling her of my New Year's Eve adventure with Brandon: how he saved my life, twice (once literally, and once my virginity). But I do take the time to tell Lisa that Brandon is my "best friend". I can't remember if I've already told her that he is also my boyfriend, or that really he is my only friend. I mean, there are his friends who I met at the party… but that's just what they are—his. Even if we do get along, they still really belong to him. I don't think they'll ever be calling me, or that I'll every be calling them. Not any time soon, anyway. They have each other; they each know who the others are. Me, I'm just Brandon's new 'friend'. For all I know, they consider me his fling. But that doesn't matter, for I know now, since New Year's Eve, that I am not just his fling. He likes me. He really does. And, I think, I really like him too— no, I know I do. And I think my liking is beginning to grow into something much more. I just hope that Brandon feels the same…

My thoughts are disrupted as Lisa asks me if I've given any more thought to trying to find ways in which to express my anger when "certain sounds occur". Or rather, I think, when someone is making them occur.

I tell her no I haven't, but I'm searching my mind to think if I actually have been putting thought into it. No—the answer is still no; I really haven't. I've definitely continued my thinking on how to avoid sounds, though. I'm always thinking about how to escape them. But to express them, no.

The only expression I seem even to be capable of is that of my feet running me out the door, the tears that flood down my cheeks, the nastiness that lashes out from behind my lips and the force of my hands whipping a dish or snapping a stick. And another thing I'd rather not mention to Lisa is the exploding of my fist as it pounds, dead center, into the side of my head. The pounding force that allows me to recover my brain's own thoughts from the repetitious sounds that overtake me and get stuck in my head. The sounds repeat themselves over and over again in my head, even when they no longer exist. The tingling in my temple tells me that they did exist, they do exist, or that they are about to begin. No, I never could tell her about all of that. I can't tell her that I hit myself; she would only try to make me stop. She'd have to, because that's her job.

Lisa asks me again if I'd like to discuss some ideas with her about how to better express my anger. I don't really want to, but my shoulders shrug an ok.

So Lisa asks me to begin. She asks me what I think I could do or say to express my feelings. Right now I feel like I want to express my feelings to her, my feelings being that this idea is dumb. Express my feelings? How could I express the feelings that overtake me in the exact moment when I am secretly wishing another person dead just because of the sound they've made? No, I can't explain any of that to her. Instead, I tell her that "I just don't see how any of this could work."

"What do you think could work for you, then?" she asks. My shoulders shrug in perplexity, but my mouth speaks.

"Well, maybe if I let people know ahead of time. I mean, before they make the sounds. I tried that with my new tutors."

Lisa's silver eyebrows lift. "Really? How'd it go?"

"Ok, I guess. I just told them that certain sounds hurt."

"But you didn't tell them about your anger." She finishes the unspoken part of my thought.

"No, not about that." I feel my breath sigh out heavily. "It's just…it's just that I don't want people to think that I'm crazy. I mean, really. Think about it. I must be crazy. I hear one little click and I burst into tears and run out of the room like a mad woman."

Lisa doesn't speak; she seems to think about what I've just said. "No, really," I continue. "You probably think I'm crazy but just won't say it, right?" my eyes demand her response.

"Jessica, you're not crazy. You just have something going on that, right now, we can't explain. That doesn't mean you're crazy."

I feel the tears forming. I don't know if I trust her words. How could she possibly deny that I am out of my mind, when even I think that I am.

"Ok, so the ear specialist didn't work out. Fine. So now you need to pick yourself back up and move on."

Tears fall.

"Are you really going to let yourself fall apart like this? Jessica, what you need to do is take control—take control over your life. I can't tell you what to do. Really, I can't make you do anything that you don't want to do. It's not up to me. It's all up to you. You alone. Do you understand that?"

I wipe away my tears. Lisa's words burn down my chest and into my stomach, a sour scolding. "I've already tried that. I tried to take control. I wanted to figure this all out, but I can't! Don't you get it? No. No, you don't. No one gets it! Not you, not me, no one!"

"Then we'll find someone who can."

"No. I'm done. No more doctors." My eyes go down. I am done: my words, this conversation, they're all done. I don't want to talk to Lisa anymore.

"Ok…let's take it slow, then."

I don't respond. "It" can move as slowly as a snail trying to slither up a Vaseline-covered slide, for all I care. I don't want to waste my time with one more doctor. I don't even know if I even want to be here with Lisa. But I am; this was part of the plan that I had supposedly once made, back in November. Back when I came home from my one week away. This part of the plan was only supposed to be part of my disguise, so I could pretend that I was letting Lisa help me. Now what? I actually am letting her help me? Yes, I have, at least somewhat. I let her send me off to Dr. Mere. I guess, at the time, it really wasn't that bad of an idea. She honestly did try to help me. Maybe I shouldn't be so cold.

"I'm sorry." My voice is small. "Sorry? For what?"

"I don't know…just for the way I am."

She smiles, "Don't be sorry for who you are, Jessica. You are you. And you know what?

You're not the anger that tries to hide itself somewhere in your head—that's not you. If it was, then you wouldn't want to get rid of it so badly. Right?"

I manage a hint of a smile. I hope that Lisa is right. I guess I'm beginning to accept having her in my life.

January: How Things Go

This surely isn't my brightest idea, but it's one that I'm forcing upon myself. I don't know why—I'm not even sure how it actually came about. Maybe it was from my last visit with Lisa. My own ridiculous words that now I'm actually making myself try out: "Maybe if I let people know ahead of time," blah, blah, blah. Did I really just randomly spurt that out? That wasn't really my plan, was it? Well, now it is. Don't ask me why, but I've just planned out my plan B to suicide: I'm approaching Mom and Dad.

We're sitting in the living room, Mom next to me and Dad across from us. They're waiting for me to talk. I mean, I did just ask them to come in here with me, right?

My hands begin to shake with just the thought of the words I will speak. But the words do come out.

"I've just been thinking…" I begin to say. "I've been thinking about everything that's been going on."

Dad interrupts, "You mean what's been going on with you?" He always comes across as being so mad. I try to ignore his tone and just focus on his words.

"Yeah, that. My headaches."

Mom: "Jess, have you been taking your medication?"

"My med…uh, yeah," I lie. That's not what I wanted to talk about. "Well, maybe it's not about my headaches. Really, it's about the sounds."

They look at each other, not speaking a word. I continue on. "I don't really have headaches. Not actual headaches, anyway. I mean, I guess it does hurt, sometimes."

"What do you mean you don't actually

have headaches? Jessica, we went to the neurologist. You told him that you do."

"No, Mom. You told him that I do."

A tingle shoots through my head. Dad's tongue has met his teeth. I try to rub the sound out of my brain. I look at Mom. She is mad.

"Jessica, it was you that told me that you do." Her eyebrows grimace down. I wait for the twitch of her eye. It comes.

I look down.

"Mom, that's only because I didn't know what else to say. I tried to tell you once before…"

"No," she cuts me off, "you never did."

"I did! I did when we were with Ms. Shay. But you both acted so weird. Why would I even want to tell you anything?"

Dad's tongue sucks his teeth. Eyes glare at me. I feel my fists clenching hard.

"Jessica, I don't remember any such thing."

"It really doesn't matter now," my words growl. He needs to stop making that sound.

SOUND

"Dad…it's that sound. Why do you always have to make that sound?"

He sucks his teeth more, and then opens his mouth, "What sound? What are you even talking about?"

I'm not sure if my fingernails have just drawn my own blood, but my palms have just been fiercely attacked.

"That sound. That sound that you make when you're mad.

That sound you make when you suck your teeth like that." Tears are pouring out now. I'm standing up, and so is Dad. We're face to face. I envision him smacking me. But he doesn't.

"What in hell are you talking about?" his voice snarls. I am his prey.

"Greg!" Mom tries a quick save. "Both of you just calm down.

Jessica, sit down."

I imagine my spit hitting him in the face. I sit.

Dad sits too. We glare; four green eyes

never showing fear, equally ready to attack.

"Greg, you do suck your teeth when you're mad." Dad's eyes zap into hers. He makes his horrible sound. I grasp the hair on the right side of my head.

Does he not even know that he's doing it? He laughs, and it's a smack in my face.

He actually finds this funny? I'm back up.

"Sit down."

"What for, to listen to you suck your teeth?" I think I may have just screamed. I did—I must have, for now Dad's voice is a roar.

"You will sit. And you will listen. You'll listen to me."

My butt finds its place on my chair. But listen? That's not about to happen here, not now. Not ever again, because he doesn't even care. He doesn't even try to listen to me. I called him here. I wanted to talk. This time was supposed to be about me, not him.

My eyes are open, but my ears are shut tight.

"I suck my teeth? That's it? That's your

excuse for your bad attitude?"

Apparently my ears are not shut tight enough. I'm full of rage, and Dad is too. There's nothing more that Mom can do. We've both gone out of control.

"It hurts me Dad, don't you understand?" I'm shouting. So is he.

"Really, Jessica? Sucking my teeth?" He sucks them hard, intentionally.

My body leaps up. I will not sit. My fists are tight. Dad laughs.

"Why don't you just deal with it? It's just a sound…" I'm gone.

"That's right! Go to your room!"

I hate him. I really, truly hate him. Why is he so mean? I might have rage, but he is just plain mean. I will never talk to him again.

Never. Not about anything. It's not just a sound. It's not… There's a small knock on my door. It's Mom. She sits down

next to me on my bed, but I don't bother to look. Why is she here? "Jessica…maybe you're right." Ok, so she got my attention.

"Maybe I haven't been listening," she continues. "I realize that I really don't know what has been happening with you. But did you ever think that maybe it's because you really haven't been telling me?"

I look into her twitching eye. I resist the urge to look away. "I know, Mom. But that's what I was just trying to do."

We study each other's faces. Mom's forehead is crinkling its stress; each and every line shows how many times I've caused her to worry.

"Would you like to talk to me now?" I'm not so sure that I do. "Will you tell me about these sounds?"

I give in; I tell her everything. Well, almost everything. I tell her all about the sounds: the clicking, the tapping, Mr. Owens' raspy voice, the sucking of teeth, and Jeffery's smacking mouth. How I can't stand to sit at the table because of the food that he smacks. That smacking sound that comes from his smacking mouth. That smacking from within his wide-open and disgusting mouth.

Mom's forehead crinkles; it tells me she really didn't want to hear all of that.

"That all makes you angry?" Her eye gives the hint of a twitch. I look away.

"I knew you wouldn't understand."

"No, Jessica—I don't. But that doesn't mean that you can't tell me about it. I just want to help."

Her arm finds its way around my shoulders. Her head rests on mine for a moment.

"I love you, Jess." She gets up and walks away.

February

Silence. White, soft silence, floating down from above. Silence. Silence that surrounds, blanketing all sound. No sound…no sound…

"Jessica! Jess! Wake up!" Mom's face is peering through the snow.

Snow? It was all a dream. My eyes are blurry; they try to focus in.

"Jess, I'm sorry. It's your Grandma." I sit up.

"Gramma?"

"Honey, she's in the hospital. Dad is waiting for me to leave.

Check that your alarm's set; you're responsible for Jeffery…" Her words sinks in.

"Wait, what?" My eyes open wide.

"Just make sure you get him on that bus. I have to go." She's already heading out.

"Mom, wait! Stop! Gramma?"

"She's ok…now. I'll call you when we hear more." She leaves. She's gone. It's 3 am. I'm wide awake. Gramma? I'll never fall back asleep tonight. I make my way downstairs; it's empty, silent as my dream. Cold as its snow. I don't want to be alone. I take my chance and call Brandon on his cell phone—no answer. I leave him a text. I pace the room, the whole downstairs: back and forth, back and forth. The memory of a thick hand grabbing hold of my shoulder overcomes me. The warmth. The strength. It turned me around, it calmed me down. Gramma. She has to be ok.

My cell is ringing. "Brandon?"

"Hey, it's me. You ok?"

I can't speak. The tears are choking me up. "Jess?"

"Gramma…"

"What? Who's there? Are you alone?"

"Yes…they're gone."

"Who's gone?"

"They're at the hospital…it's my Gramma." "I'm coming over."

The line is dead.

I pace the floor. My phone suffocates inside my palm; I drop it to the floor. My legs give out, and I'm on the floor. She has to be ok.

…Now, they're here. Brandon and Sharron. I'm in his arms. "Is she ok?" I hear Brandon's voice.

"I don't know," Sharron says. I've soaked Brandon's shirt with my tears. "They said they'd call." He holds me tightly.

"Come on Brandon, come in here and sit her down." It's Sharron. Brandon brings me to where she is in the living room.

Sharron grabs Mom's fleece off the back of the couch. "Lay her down." She points to the sofa, directing Brandon.

He lays me down. I don't want to sleep—my mind is numb.

Brandon is rubbing the side of my cheek

softly.

"Go to sleep..." His voice is calm. But my eyes keep wide open. "We can't stay too long," Sharron says. "Dad will have my head."

"When's he coming back?" Brandon asks. "I don't know, 6:30?"

"Where is he?" my voice crawls out.

"He's doing the night shift," Sharron informs me. "He'd kill me if he knew I drove Brandon here."

I put my head back down, still numb. I just want to know that Gramma's ok.

"Jess?" It's Sharron, "we spoke to your parents; they said they'd call. Now go to sleep. We're here; everything's going to be alright."

I'm not alone. My eyes close, head, still numb. Heavy...numb... gone...

Dinner is set all around Gramma's table, with her special china, her hand sewn lace napkins, each set in their perfect place. Music plays softly from the other room. I hear everyone talking, laughing, having fun.

I walk into the room, but there's no one

there…they're gone. But where? They were just there. The music has turned off. Something's wrong.

I turn; I run back into the dining room. It's empty—no food. The china, the napkins…all gone.

"Gramma!" My voice echoes my fear. "Gramma!" No one is here… the phone is ringing…I don't know where it is.

"Hello?" it's Jeffery's voice…

"Mommy? Where are you?" It's Jeffery on our phone. I'm awake, and he's handing me the phone. I clear my voice.

"Mom?"

"Hi, Jess. You got Jeffery up?"

"Um, yes." No reason to admit that he just woke me. "How's Gramma?" I feel really strange just waking from that dream.

"We're still waiting to see…they've been running a lot of tests…she's in ICU." Mom's voice is tired. I wish I were there with her.

"What's an ICU?"

"Intensive Care Unit. They're keeping a

good eye on her." "What happened?"

"Something with her stomach." Her voice sounds sick. "They may have found something..."

"What do you mean?"

"In her pancreas...a growth. They want to biopsy it, I think." We're silent.

"Jess, I'll call you when we know more. Just get Jeffery on that bus, and don't worry about your class. I don't know when we'll be back. Just call Ms. Mackie; it's Monday, right?"

"Yeah, right. Ok. Call me, Mom." She hangs up.

It's just me and Jeffery at home. He'll want to eat. I'll want to die. I point him away, telling him to go get dressed. He begs me to come: "...but I'm scared all alone!"

I go with him. At least there's no food, not yet.

Jeffery is getting dressed, flaunting his style of mismatched clothes, his Spiderman shirt clashing loudly with a pair of funky pants.

"Jeffery, where's your brush?" His hair is a

mess; I'll have to water it down for sure.

"No! I'm not brushing my hair!" He runs away.

Great. There's no way I'm chasing him; I'll just get him fed and send him on his way.

He's already downstairs, pulling a chair up to the cabinet. His short little arms reach up high, but not quite high enough,

"Jessica, help!"

"Jeffery, get down!" I sound just like Mom. "I'll get it. Go pick out your cereal."

He grabs a box and I fill his bowl. I place it down and walk away, quickly.

"I'm just getting dressed!" I shout.

Then I run, up the stairs to the safety of my room, safely away from the sounds of his chewing. I'm relieved that he doesn't try to call me back down.

Finally, he's on the bus. He smiles as I wave him down the street. I could almost smile back, but I don't. I can only think of Gramma. I hope Mom calls me back soon.

She doesn't, but I see that Brandon has

made his way back

here.

"You didn't go to school?" I ask. He grins.

"Why, were you expecting me to?" True. For him, this is nothing new.

"You really should start going to school more often." I wince. Taking care of Jeffery really does turn me into Mom. Brandon smiles.

"Are you ok? Did you hear anything new?"

"No, not yet. Just that it's something with her stomach. Her pancreas."

"Oh…" His voice is strange. "What?"

"Oh, nothing. I just hope she's ok." He smiles strangely, but pulls me in for a hug. I know that he's thinking of something more, but I don't pry for an answer. I'm just glad that he's here and that Jeffery is gone.

Brandon stays with me throughout the whole morning and into the afternoon, distracting me, holding me, making me laugh. Then Mom calls. She's on her way home with Dad. They've moved Gramma out of the ICU and into her own room, and they're coming home to get me so I can go see her. Mariana will babysit Jeffery when he gets out of school.

Brandon is getting ready to leave. He needs to go before my parents get back; I'd be grounded for a month if they ever caught us alone together in this house.

We're standing outside on the top of Grandpa's steps. Brandon is kissing me on the lips, softly. I feel how he doesn't want to go. My words find a break in his kiss.

"Brandon…thanks for being here." But my hands won't let him go—not yet. I pull him back in and he kisses me some more.

"I'd better go. I'll see you later, Jess."

He turns to leave. I feel the words as they flow unexpectedly from my mouth.

"I love you." I say this to him for the very first time. The words have been released, freely forming their waves and traveling out onto the breeze.

Brandon turns back around, his eyes aglow. "What did you say?"

My head shies down. My cheeks are red.

"I love you, Brandon."

He's lifting up my chin so my eyes can meet his. There's a smile on his lips.

"I love you too, Jessica." Our mouths attach. I never want to let him go.

But I must, for he has to go.

Dad's eyes are red. This is the first time I have looked into them in probably a month but I can't feel the hate now. Our pain has made our frustration break. We've come back together, at least for now. For Gramma. But I know it won't last, and I'm sure he knows it as well.

Gramma lies inclined upward, two pillows propped beneath her head.

"My sweet Jessie," she says. Her words are soft.

"Hi Gramma." I sit on the side of her bed. I'm scared to touch her arm; there's a taped needle and tube coming out of it that feeds an awkward looking bag filled with a clear liquid. The bag hangs from what looks like a miniature coat rack.

Gramma watches the direction of my eyes and forms a rounded smile.

"Oh, that. Ugly old thing, isn't it? They say it hydrates me. I say just give me a drink! Those nurses—they're all crazy!" She lets out a laugh, but grasps her stomach in tightly with one hand.

"Come here, come give me my hug." This time it's me who holds her, but not too tightly. I'm scared I'll hurt her and she'll pretend she's alright.

We don't stay long, but it's good to hear Gramma laugh. She says she's having the biopsy done later in the day. She demands that Mom and Dad to go home and sleep, and that I give Jeffery a big ounce of all her lovin' for her. Surely she can't be talking just to me. No way, I think. Getting Jeffery ready for school was more than enough for today—more than enough for an entire year! I feel my lips smile as we walk away down the hall. I hope the biopsy shows that Gramma will be ok.

It doesn't. The biopsy is bad—really bad. I can tell by the look on Dad's face, which is swollen and red. I don't remember if I've ever seen him cry before, but now I know that this is what it's like. This is the day that I hear the words come out of his mouth that I never wanted to hear. Gramma has cancer. She only has a few months left to live.

I can't move. I can't feel my legs. My eyes are stuck, stuck staring at Dad's. His eyes are red, bloodshot, and swollen. Mine are dripping wet.

"I'm sorry, Jessica." His arms wrap around my body, squeezing me tightly. The kind of hug he must have learned from Gramma. Gramma's hug. I can't breathe. I can't escape. I don't care that I said I'd hate Dad—I hug him back. I feel him crying; he lets his sadness release.

His tears are falling; they mix down on top of my head. "I'm so sorry…Dad."

February: Coping

I'm here again with Lisa. We missed our last appointment due to all that's been going on with Gramma. But here I am again, and again Lisa's eyes look concerned. I am a mess. With all the added stress, each and every sound has become that much more painful. The little tolerance I'd had is gone, and now a new sound has begun torturing me, one that I can't escape. How can I? It's the sound of breathing—a deep breath, an exaggerated breath, a sighing breath. I mean, people do have to breathe, right? I can't just ask them to stop. I can't just say, "please don't breathe," just so that I won't die. And so this is how it is:

their death or mine. Of course, it will always be mine.

I try to describe to Lisa what has been going on, even though I can tell it doesn't make any sense to her. I watch the rigid motion of her fingers—they're tense. She's resisting her natural nervous tic, her urge to tappity-tap. I think that's how she concentrates, but with me all concentration comes to a halt.

I listen to my words as they shift over to Gramma. They're telling Lisa how I don't want Gramma to go. I don't want her to die.

Gramma is the only one who understands what I mean about the sounds, how I hate them, how I want them to stop. But no…it's not so much Gramma who understands—it was Grandpa. Gramma gave me the earplugs to wear because they had helped him…

"Earplugs? Your Grandpa wore earplugs?" Lisa breaks in. "Yeah, when he ate with Gramma. At least, that's what she

says."

"Earplugs." She smiles. "And you tried

them out? How did it

go—did it work?"

"I guess...sort of. I sat through the meal. But that's only because Gramma was there."

"Are you sure?" She pauses. "You don't think they could help again?"

"I don't know. I wouldn't even know where to buy them." "Hmm..."

I hate that sound. I look away. But Lisa doesn't notice; she continues on.

"Well, I can't exactly prescribe earplugs for you to wear, as a prescription that is. But, I could write your mom a little note if you're willing to give them another try."

I look back up. I guess it couldn't hurt—nothing could hurt me like the sounds themselves. So I let Lisa write the note and give it to Mom.

Mom looks at it and tucks it in her purse. I see her lips mouth the word, "earplugs," but nothing comes out. Apparently she has taken it into consideration, though, because she takes me to CVS. The pharmacist points us to the correct aisle. There are lots of different kinds of earplugs. But then I see purple ones.

"This one." I grab the box from the shelf. Mom looks it over.

"I guess they should work." She brings the box to the counter and pays. I'm already starting to feel a bit of relief, even just feeling the box swinging down around my wrist inside the plastic CVS bag. I can only hope that the earplugs really will help, even just a little. Anything, any bit, just to help me to escape from the sounds.

*

Frozen sticks crack between frozen dirt and feet. Four feet sneak out into the dark, into the night. They follow a flashlight's flicker that barely reaches ahead, into the thickness of the tangled, leafless twigs. We follow the path, Brandon and I, the path to our secret place. The way to our little house. It's cold—it's freezing. Where is the snow? I wonder. But there's no time to think about it, at least not

now. Brandon's hand grips mine, pulling

me to match his speed. We're running fast, and the speed fills us quickly with heat. Brandon has something for me, he says; he'll show me when we get to our house.

Something in his eyes hints that I shouldn't have followed him here. But I did. It's Valentine's Day and I wouldn't have spent it any other way. And now we're here…

Brandon opens the door ahead of me, telling me to wait. He's lighting the lantern and turning off the flashlight.

"Come in." His eyes glow; he is a wolf in the dark of the night.

I follow him inside. He's been here and been busy, I see. An oversized bean chair, blankets and pillows, and up on top of the log table is a red cloth rose in a little vase. I smile. He's looking at me sweetly. Sweet with mischief, but sincerely sweet.

"You like it?" He's pulling me in and sitting me close. He pulls the blanket up to cover us up, folding our bodies together into a cocoon.

"I love it," I say, although I feel a little

nervous. I suspect that I know now why he has brought me here. But then again, maybe I'm wrong.

Brandon reaches into the small bag he has brought along with us and pulls out a thermos.

"Hot chocolate," he grins. I feel a little silly as he begins pouring some for me and then for himself.

But the hot chocolate isn't all—Brandon is taking something else out of his bag as well. He places it down and smoothes it out: a miniature piece of paper. He reaches back in the bag for something more, finds it, and sprinkles it down on top of the paper. On top of the paper the sprinkles transform into something thick: a line straight down the center. I see little dry leaves all lined in a row, being lined

and rolled. Brandon pinches the end and gives it a twist; he lights it up as it's pinched to his lips. He breathes it in, but doesn't breathe it out.

His hand is guiding the paper toward me…

I want to say no, but not even that will come out of my mouth; my lips are frozen shut. I'm think back to Abby, how we swore our little oath: we will never touch the stuff. Now, it's only my head that manages to speak, with a little shake back and forth.

Brandon breathes back out, but smiles. He doesn't seem bothered, as his mind is apparently somewhere else

"Jess, I've been thinking." Our eyes meet. "About your gramma." He breathes in some more, looks away, and breathes it out again.

That sound. I try to block it out.

Brandon doesn't speak. He seems to have forgotten what he was going to say. Then, he remembers.

"Really, about my mom. I was five when she got sick."

His eyes are squinting. He breathes in more; he breathes it out again.

I rub my head. All I want to hear is his

words, so why is all my ears hear that sound? Brandon goes on.

"After she was gone, I used to have these dreams. You know, that she was still there. I'd wake up and I'd just start crying…" He stops there. I can't tell if he's crying now. His eyes seem red, but at the same time dry. No, I realize, he's high. Really high. And even I'm starting to have a hard time focusing. My head is turning light. I watch Brandon's hand; it moves the paper very slowly up to his lips. He breathes in, holds it, and breathes it out. The sound. The sound was there. It was there. I heard it in my head and I wanted to be mad. But maybe, maybe I'm not…

The air. It's the air. His smoke is filling the air, filling our little house, filling my lungs. My brain is numb; my rage is numb. I put out my hand and Brandon hands me the rolled up paper. I breath it in; it burns. I choke it out, and Brandon laughs. I laugh too. Rage is numb…

I'm not sure how we make it back to Brandon's house, but we do. We even make it on time. But Sharron has us all figured out.

"Oh shit, Brandon." Her eyes send silent curses into his. "I can't send her home like this."

She grabs me by my hand and drags me up the stairs, "You have to change. I smell it all over your clothes. You'll have to wear mine.

And your eyes—! Did he talk you into this?"

I don't answer. It's all happening too quickly. Everything's still fuzzy; my brain is not thinking too clearly just yet.

Sharron's face is in my hair. I feel her inhaling my scent. "No, this won't work. Your hair's holding in the smell. Get in the

shower. Wash it out."

I feel confused, but I do what she says. The shower seems to help—clearer thoughts are coming back. It numbed my rage. I made it through the night: I heard the sound of Brandon's breath, but the rage was numbed out. It was indeed, but so was everything else. I'm not sure I really liked it. I mean, it did feel good—we had a lot of fun. But how could it be good when I had no idea what was going on? I don't like being out of control of myself and my own thoughts. It was no different than my rage, taking me over, burying my thoughts. It took away my right to have the thoughts that I wanted to have: thoughts that are clear, thoughts that make sense, thoughts that I actually want to think. It may have helped me to cope, but it wasn't what I want. I don't want it like that.

March

Gramma's hands are no longer thick. She's here. She came for my birthday, my Sweet 16. Thinned arms give me a gentle squeeze.

"My sweet Jessie," her voice smiles. I imagine her cheeks rounding out, forming their pink, warm circles as she smiles. But the circles are not there. Her cheeks are no longer fat. I long for her suffocating hug—I would fall into it and never resist. But it will not come. Her strength is gone, although her eyes still flicker with her life. I focus into them. They let me know who she is, that she is still here. Gramma. I will not let her go.

"What's this?" she's asking me; she's wiping away the tear that has escaped down my cheek. I force a smile.

"Just glad you're here, Gramma."

She smiles back and wraps her hand over the top of my shoulder. I help her to the couch. She is sick.

Brandon is sitting in the living room with my family. He is watching me as I help Gramma into the room, and I feel her eyes watching him too. It's the first time that they've met.

"Gramma, this is my friend Brandon."

She smiles and calls him a "handsome young man."

I'm not sure, but I think I see a slight blush on his cheeks. He stands, taking her hand in his, and shakes it warmly. I wonder if his eyes make hers melt, as they do mine.

Gramma gives me a discrete little nod of the head, accompanied by a wink. A small laugh escapes my lips, as her laugh escapes from her own mouth. My mind erases the fact that that she is sick. Today, from this moment on, I will not let that thought exist. Today we are going to have fun.

And we do. But soon I need to make my escape. I sneak into the bathroom and put my plan into place: little purple earplugs. Mom is getting ready for my cake. I can't let the rage happen—I won't let it happen. I won't let myself feel the rage. I won't…

But it is here—of course it is here, along with Jeffery as he smacks his cake. How can one smack cake? It's not even wet—it's cake! Even with the earplugs in place, even with the sound almost completely muffled, the rage is here. I feel it. I feel it seeping over the expression on my face. I feel my fists clenching tightly, one on my fork, the other rising to the side of my face. To my ear. To my hair, wanting to rip it out. That smack. It won't go away…

"Jessie." It's Gramma. "Jessie, look here."

I see her eyes. They tell me to let the rage release. Let it release into her warm eyes.

I can't. It's too late. My head shakes 'no'.

I run away…

I didn't want it to be like that, my last birthday with Gramma. I wanted her to see me ok. I wanted her to know that I was going to be alright. I wanted her to believe the lie that I tried to force on myself.

But I guess she would have known that it wasn't true. She lived it a long part of her life, with Grandpa. But still, I wanted me to be different. I wanted her to see that I could defeat this thing, this rage that sneaks its way into my head. This rage that makes no logical sense.

This rage that overtakes my every thought, that makes me insane.

Why?

I'm telling Lisa all about my birthday with Gramma. All about the cake, about the smacking of the cake and about the failure of the purple ear plugs. They didn't work—they muffled the sound, but not the rage. Why do I have to have such rage? It doesn't even make sense.

Every day it is getting worse. Every day I can deal with it less. Every chance I get I make my escape into my room. I lock my door; I pound my head; I create new pain so that the pain of rage will stop. I don't tell Lisa—I don't even let Brandon know. Even though he knows everything else, I could never tell him about my self-inflicted pain.

Like Lisa, he would only try to make me stop. But I can't stop. Hurting myself is the only thing that helps. It's the only thing that makes my rage come to an end quickly. The rage comes in, I pound it out, and my thoughts come back—the thoughts that I want to have.

I wonder if maybe Brandon is crazy right along with me. I mean, how could he even want to be with someone like me, someone who snaps instantly out of nowhere, snapping into an uncontrollable rage? Someone who hurts herself in order to take the rage away? Even if he doesn't know exactly what I do, still, he must be crazy to be with someone as crazy as me. But through it all, he's also the only one who keeps me sane, who makes me want to live another day, although I don't know how much longer that will even last. I feel my will to live shrinking away fast.

March: Spring

How is it spring when it was never winter? The grass did die; the air did freeze; the leaves were gone. But winter was never really here. It tried to come early, once back in the fall and again in the beginning of March three days before my birthday, but that was it. Winter showed its face and then faded away, seeping into the ugly, frozen death of the earth. The earth exposed and uncovered like me.

The earth, never quite finding its soft, comforting blanket. And when Winter did decide to wrap itself over me, it faded away just as quickly, re-exposing my ugly instability, my death by insanity.

Now the seasons are separating themselves from me. I no longer fit into their cycle with the earth. The first purple flower is popping its lively little self out from the death of the ground; the earth is coming back to life. It's taking its own death and creating something new, but I am not. I remain dead. My dying will not nourish another being into life; I have no dormant seed within my being, waiting to sprout into life. My death is final.

Death has swallowed my life. Within one year's gulp, rage has brought me to death—the death of my sanity, the death of my friendship with Abby, the death of school. And, soon, the death of my family. Gramma has moved into our den. She can no longer take care of herself. Hospice has given us a hospital bed for her to use…until she is gone. I want to die with her. I want to bring my self-torture to an end. My death brings forth no purple flower. I am fully dead. So why does my body bother to breathe, to take in air or pump blood throughout my veins? There is no point. I do have Brandon, but he deserves better. He deserves to be with someone who is alive, someone who can continue to live. I can only die again and again, each day, with each and every sound that grinds the insides of my brain. Sounds that really aren't that bad, at least, not to anyone else—just to me. And they kill me. I would be better off dead...truly dead. And so that is what I will be. This time, no one will stop me...

My stomach is erupting, flaming upward through a volcanic tube, up through my chest, up into my throat, and blazing out from my mouth through the other end of the tube that's been forced into my chest. I am awake, and I am alive. My stomach has been pumped. I failed to die.

Mom is rubbing my back. Tears fill her eyes.

Why didn't I just die? I want to be dead.

Mom tells me to go to sleep. We'll talk when I wake. Why do I have to come back awake?

As I wake, though, she is no longer here. But Brandon is. He's rubbing my head, smoothing the locks away from my eyes, eyes that are starting to cry.

"I just wanted to die," I tell him.

"No," he says. "No, you can't." He won't let me.

I tell him that he shouldn't be with me, that he deserves better.

He says that's a lie, that he won't go—he'll never go. I'm stuck with him until he dies, which, he informs me, is not happening any time soon.

A doctor is walking in with Mom and Dad. Brandon has to leave. He tells me that he will be back. He kisses me softly on the top of my head.

The doctor is going over my chart, but I'm not really listening.

Mom and Dad can handle that. What I do know is, is they're going to force me to get help. As soon as I'm up on my feet, I'm going away again for another week's stay. At least a week, they say, until

my depression is under control. They realize now that I've only been pretending to take my medication. And now, I will be given no choice. They will watch me swallow it down. They're starting me over; they're taking control. My life is no longer my own. But who cares? I am already dead inside.

The medication is not right. I think I am back at our little house, high with Brandon, for my thoughts are not my own. I am not myself. They say I will have to try something else. I don't want to try anything else. I want this to end—I want to go home. They say that's not possible, not until my medication is right.

And so here I am, stuck. Stuck without a fight. There's no point in a fight. While I'm here, I have no rights.

And so I give in. Well, a little bit anyway: I tell them again about the sounds, how certain sounds hurt my head and take away my thoughts, how they fill me with rage, how they make me want to end my life.

They don't care. To them, that's just a 'reaction', my reaction to stress and anxiety. And on top of that, they have a new theory: OCD. They feel that I have an obsession with sound. That sound does not actually 'hurt' me. But I know that it does—it kills me! It kills my sanity; it fills me with rage. But they are not interested in what I have to say.

So I ask, "If I do have OCD, then what is my compulsion?" To run away? One doctor actually listens. He suggests that maybe it's Pure-O OCD. That is, OCD, but without the compulsion. That makes a little sense, I guess. But it still doesn't explain my brain's reaction, the reaction that comes directly from the sounds. Or maybe it's that a signal in my brain has gone completely wrong?

Really, I don't care. I just want to go home. I don't want their medications. I don't want their labels. What I have is nothing that they could ever understand. My brain is its own; I am alone. There is nothing for them to find out. Just let me go. But no, they won't—they keep me here. They stamp me with their book-discovered labels again and again. With their labels comes the drugs. Drugs that, this time, are forced straight down my throat.

Did you hear me? I said no!

April

Three weeks of Hell and I am finally home. Friday the 13th… hopefully not a bad omen. I don't wish to die any longer, so I guess that's good. At least everyone else got their wish. And I got mine: Gramma is still here. I didn't want to come home to find her gone. But still, she is not well. Her doctor said that it will be any time now. She can't get out of bed; her skin and eyes are yellow; her liver is failing.

I have come home just in time to watch her die, a death I had wished for myself.

I approach Gramma slowly. Her yellow eyes watch me from her thin, yellow face. Her body is a skeleton—she looks so frail. I sit in the chair that's been placed close to her bed, and I take her hand carefully into mine.

"My sweet Jessie…" A weak voice climbed its way out of her throat.

"Gramma." I can't help the tears that flow down from my eyes. I don't want her to die. I can't ever let her go. And I really, really hope she doesn't know where I've been the past couple weeks. But she does.

"Oh, Jessie." I feel the squeeze of her hand, "Promise me to not do that again."

I can't speak. I can only stare through my tears into the yellow eyes that are supposed to be hers. They are hers…but something has broken them down, colored them over with yellow chalk. A little smile emerges from Gramma's lips.

"But if you do decide to do that again, Jessie," she says, and pauses, making sure that I hear her clearly, "and if you succeed, I'll hunt you down Up There."

"I'm so sorry, Gramma." And really, I am. Not so much for me, but for what it must have been like for her, knowing, being so sick and stuck here worrying about me. What was I thinking, leaving her like that?

"Don't be sorry. Just be strong." I'm not sure how to interpret the pain in her tone; is it for me, or is it for her? Probably both. I feel guilt pushing down hard on my heart. Gramma continues speaking.

"Your grandpa, now, he was strong. He didn't give in to those sounds." She stops for a moment, a grimace creeping over her face. I don't interrupt. "They hurt him, you know, just like they hurt you.

Don't you think you've ever been alone—he's Up There watching over you." One hand holds her stomach, the other squeezes my hand. "Yes he is. And I will be too." A single tear drips down from her yellow eye.

I don't want Gramma to die. But I know that she soon will.

*

Gramma is gone. Her body is still here, but she is gone. She died in Dad's arms. He gave her the morphine and they both fell asleep, his head lying by her side, his arm wrapped over her waist, her hand resting gently on his head and her fingers woven into the curls of his hair. She did not wake up. She will never wake up. She is gone.

Jeffery is crying. Mom is holding him on her lap. Uncle Gary, Aunt Sandy, Sarah, and Gavin are on their way. Dad is still next to Gramma. My eyes can't look at her lifeless body, but I walk up slowly behind Dad. I don't have any words; my hand finds its way to his shoulder and he turns. He's looking into my eyes. Our eyes reflect each other's pain for the death of our dear one. My gramma; his mom. The pain has made us both numb—neither can cry and neither can speak. Our eyes tell each other what our mouths cannot. We embrace in a hug, the hug that we have learned from Gramma. In her death she has brought us back together. In our new connection, she is alive. I feel her; she's watching over us. There's a spark in her now clear eyes.

*

Jeffery and I have said goodbye to Gramma. We're leaving the wake separately; he's going home with Mariana and I'm leaving with Brandon and his dad. Mom and Dad will stay until everyone else has left.

It's the first time I've seen Brandon since he told me he would be back. He never did make it, at least not while I was still there in the hospital. By the time he came back for me I was already gone, and they had swept me away for my three week stay.

Everything from that moment on has moved so slowly, yet at the same time so fast. My life had been set on slow motion, while Gramma's leapt ahead. All that I didn't want to deal with, all that I tried to fight, had endlessly dragged on. And then, BAM! Gramma was gone, right when they finally decided I was finally stable enough to go back home.

Of course, it was all my own fault—there's no taking it back. I did what I did. I tried to end my life, and now I will be forever stuck with the consequences. I missed the last three weeks of Gramma's life. I missed all that was left of her life just because I wanted to take away my own.

Brandon is quiet as his dad drives us to their house. His eyes barely meet mine. If it wasn't for his hand holding mine, I would think that he's upset at me.

His dad has dropped us off at their house, and we're alone with Sharron. She gives me a hug and tells me she's glad I'm ok, that I better never try that again, and that she's "so sorry about your Gramma."

Brandon tells her that we're going upstairs and that she shouldn't follow us. She lets us go. I guess she figures that with all that's happened, there's no need for us to keep the door open. Nothing is about to happen, not now. So she lets us go.

We're sitting on Brandon's bed, both silent. But his arm is tight around me; he's holding me close.

"Jessica, I love you." The words escape his lips.

I look up into the moisture of his brown eyes; they're looking back down into my green ones. I feel them seeping into mine, flowing up into my mind, into my thoughts, into me. He's feeling out who I am and who I have become. Does he really love me? I'm not sure if I trust his words, but I respond.

"I love you, too." And really, I do. Whether his words are true or not, mine are.

"Then don't ever do that again." His voice is firm. And strange.

I not only hurt my family, I also hurt him.

My tears are starting to flow. My numbness has found its break.

I feel it now, what a horrible person I am. "I'm so sorry, Brandon…I'm so sorry."

"Then don't do it again," he repeats. His eyes burn into me. "You come to me instead—you don't go there again." His hands are grasping the sides of my face, hard. It hurts, but I don't care. I hear a whisper trickle out through my tears.

"I won't. I won't do it again."

Brandon lets go of my face. I feel the marks of his hands still there, red-hot prints. But they can't equal to what I've done to him. He should hurt me more—I want him to. I wouldn't care. I let my body collapse into his. Why didn't I go to him? He will never be able to look at me the same way again.

May

Every week I now meet with Lisa. Every day I take my medications. Mom and Dad take turns: they stand, they watch, they make sure I swallow it all down. I think the medication is helping a little, even though I still hate the sounds. But at least I haven't had the urge to kill myself, and I am a little less anxious, although I still have to fight the urge to hit my head. And, I have slipped. How couldn't I?

The sounds, they still come. How could they not? People do have to breathe, eat, and not let their snot drip out. Spring is here; pollen's in the air; people are bound to sniffle it up. Why not just blow it out? That, I can't figure out—

why people have to be so gross. Why they have to make that sniffling sound. Just get it out!

That is exactly what I feel like screaming at Ms. Mackie. She has seasonal allergies and her sniffling never comes to an end. I can

hardly concentrate. My grades have dropped in both of her classes. She doesn't understand what is happening, though. She told me, way back, to let her know if she's making a sound that is bothering me. But how do I tell her that? How do I tell her, in the moment of rage, when all I feel like is ripping off her head? I spend the whole four hours, two for English and two for Social Studies, clenching and yanking the little locks of hair that are unfortunate enough to reside over my ears. Luckily for them, I have yet to yank them out, but I still can't tolerate Ms. Mackie's sniffling.

She, too, has become very frustrated with me, and she has let it be known. She said that I need to start focusing and doing my work. I told her that "I'd rather just do it at home." And so that is what I do now. We meet at the library, seemingly for me to just glare at her. We sit. She sniffs. I grasp my hair. She corrects my homework and assigns me some more, and then I pretend to read while she corrects my homework. This goes on for four whole hours, with only a half-hour break in between. Our time spent together is pointless, other than the fact that it pays Ms. Mackie's salary. But for me, it's an absolute waste of time, a waste of my sanity. And my fists, they just clench and wait. They wait to be able to explode onto the side of my head…and hers,

I imagine with satisfaction. But I can never actually do it—I can only imagine. And I know my wrath must come to a stop sooner or later. And so I've given it a lot of thought. I can't make myself stop, but I know who can. Brandon. At least, I think he can. He can help me control my reactions, or so I hope. He does know how to calm me down; he does know how to tame my rage. He makes me stop my insanity; he waits, and soon my rage goes away. He did tell me I had better go to him if something is wrong. And so I will.

Brandon comes over to my house—I have called him here. I'm ready to tell him the something that he won't want to hear: how I've been hitting my head. We're alone in my room with the door barely cracked open. But it's open enough so that no one will peek in or enter uninvited.

Brandon has picked up on the fact that I don't want to share with him what I'm about to say.

"Whatever it is, Jess, it's ok to tell me." He's rubbing my back. It helps me to almost relax.

I ask him if he remembers the stick that he broke at our little house. He smiles a bit sly, saying that he does. Then he waits for me to go on.

"Do you remember grabbing my hands?" My eyes find their way down. My hands shake.

He lifts my chin back up and says, "I do. You hit your head." My words feel jumbled, but

I let them fall out.

"I can't stop."

Brandon's smile is gone. But he doesn't look mad—maybe a little bit scared, but not mad.

"You can't stop?"

"Hitting myself, Brandon. I want to stop. I want you to stop me."

He takes both of my hands, feeling them shake. He's taking my fear away, making it his.

"How?"

"I don't know, Brandon. But please, make me stop. Please."

He pulls me into his arms and tells me it's alright. He doesn't know how, but he will help me to stop. He'll find a way.

We sit together, his arms around me. Neither of us speak.

If only I could read what's inside of his head—I want to hear his thoughts, what his thoughts of me are. I wish I could take back all of the things that I've just said. What does he think of me now, I wonder? He already knew that I'm crazy…but now? How does he see me now? I wonder how much longer he'll even want to be with me now that he knows I keep hitting my head. He must think I'm even more than just crazy; he must think I'm a crazy psychopath. First I try to kill myself, he must be thinking, and now this?

"Brandon, it's ok if you want to leave me. I'll understand." The words have snuck out before I could make them stop. They shock me, but they seem to have shocked him even more so.

"What?" He forces my body up, adjusting my face and riveting my eyes straight into his. "Leave you? Jessica, I'm not going to leave you—I want to help you."

And they're here again, the tears that love to find my face. How many times must he witness this? I am a wreck.

"Why would you even want to help me? I can never be fixed."

Brandon is silent. Is this it? His eyes are not those of a wolf anymore, they're like those of a bear. They're fierce. I am scared.

But Brandon is not scared. He is taking control; he's doing now what I had hoped he would.

"Jessica, I love you. And I don't care if you're ever fixed or not. But, you will get better. And you are not going to hit your head anymore.

I'm not going to let you. Do you understand that?"

I can't answer because he's gripping my face, but he releases it as his lips touch mine.

He gives me no choice. It was what I had wanted him to do: take control. But he says that I need to take control, too, that it won't work unless I do. He will help me, but I also have to help myself. And so we put together our plan for me. When the rage arises, he will come to me. I cannot be alone; I have to give him a call. I don't have to speak, I only have to listen to him. He'll stay there on the other line until I am calm. If I need him here, he will come. He'll find a way. He lets me know: he is here, and I don't have to be alone.

So, for now, I don't feel so alone. But as to the twistedness inside my head, I am. Brandon is here for me, but does he really understand? How could he? In many ways I am still very alone.

May: This is Me

My cell is ringing somewhere near my head—under my pillow.

It wakes me up.

"Hello?"

"Jess!" It's Brandon.

"Hey, what time is it?" I'd rather not focus my eyes enough to see.

"Six." Brandon answers.

"Six am? Ugh, Brandon, it's Saturday." I hear him laugh.

"Jess, did you watch ABC's 20/20 last night?" "20/20? No."

"Jessica. Get up."

He's making me mad. I just want to go

back to bed. But I sit up reluctantly.

"Why? What?" Brandon laughs again.

"It's worth it, Jess. You have to look something up. Go get online.

Look up Misophonia." "Miso-what?" I'm annoyed.

"Misophonia. Just do it—I'll be there as soon as I can." He hangs up. This had better be good, I think.

I'm looking this strange word up, trying to google it. There it is. I click on a link and I'm reading the words. "The hatred of sound." The hatred of sound? Chills race up my spine. I read some more…it's all there: the sniffling, the breathing, the clicking, and the smacking. It's all there! Even the certain tones of voice, like Mr. Owens'. It is all here. This is me, I think. I'm not alone. I'm not alone!

With that I'm leaping off my bed, and then just as quickly sitting back down. I'm clicking another link. I've found a whole group—a whole group of people like me. Just like me. A forum. I start to read, and the words I read are my words. My thoughts. All of the things that make up my problem, being explained by them. They know my words; they know my thoughts; they know me. And I know them. I am not alone. I am not crazy, and I feel such relief.

"I'm not crazy!" I hear it out loud. It has shouted out from my mouth. I hear my own sound: I'm not crazy. My tears are falling down. My lips are turning up in a grin. I am not crazy, and I am not alone.

I can't stop reading. I'm reading everyone's posts. It's all about me: me and them and this thing called Misophonia. We are one.

*

Lisa looks surprised as I walk into her office. It's a Monday, and even more strangely, a smile is taking over my face. It quickly spreads to hers, however.

"What's going on?" she asks.

I hand her the paper I've printed out from the Misophonia website, a letter that is written for doctors to describe what I have. This letter will tell her of what I have been trying to describe with no success. Well, maybe I did have a little success, as she never questioned whether my words were true or not. But now, now I have proof. What I have is real and not only happening inside of my head, for there's a whole group. A group that is forming and growing. A group of people with Misophonia that are coming together, and we're all saying, "This is me. This is what I have. I really am not crazy after all."

Lisa's face is beaming.

"Jessica, this is amazing. How did you find it?"

I tell her it was Brandon, and explain how he saw it on a show. "This is great. So now, where would you like to go from here?" I feel my mind stop. From here? I hadn't really thought of that.

The website says that Misophonia is something new. Well, not new because it hasn't been around, but new because it's just recently been recognized. There's really not much anyone can do. At the moment, hardly any research exists. I feel the sudden upheaval of a familiar dread. There isn't anywhere for me to go. There's really nothing that anyone can do... I'm suddenly at a loss for words.

"I don't know."

Lisa notices my sudden change. "I'm not trying to bring you down. I'm just wondering what I can do to help."

"Help? I don't know. It says there's not a lot anyone can do. It does mention the ear plugs, though." I feel a little smile sneak its way back. Lisa smiles too.

"I would really like to learn more about this, Jessica. Do you mind if I take this letter home?"

I let her keep it—that's what it was for. Anyway, everything on it is already written, in permanent ink, all over the inside of my head. It is all there. Now I know I'm really not crazy. I no longer have that fear.

But Lisa has brought up a good point:

even though the fear may be gone, the sounds are not. They're still there; they're still everywhere, although, these past few days I've seemed to notice them less. Yet even though the sounds are still there, I am not quite the same mess I was. Yes, I do still flee the room, and yes, I do fight back my tears, but I have been recovering much more quickly, and I have yet to hit my head since I learned about Misophonia. Since I learned that I am not alone.

Lisa breaks back through my thoughts. "Have you told your parents yet?" My parents?

"No." I have no idea how to do that. "I'm not so sure I'm ready just yet."

"No?"

"I don't know. I just don't think that they'll believe it. Well, maybe Mom…but Dad…there's just no way." My mind is quickly crumbling and bringing me back to reality. "It's just a sound!" Dad's words hurt me badly even after all this time. He has hurt me badly; he hasn't even tried to understand. Sure, we've been a little closer since Gramma passed away, but still, I have nothing to say to him about this new discovery. There's nothing that I want to say. Not to him.

And maybe that's just it—maybe I don't have to say a word.

There is another letter on the site, a letter for families. I'll print it tonight and leave it on my parents' bed before I go to sleep. They'll have the whole night to think about it while I am sleeping safe and sound. They won't wake me, at least I don't think they will. We can talk in the morning after the night lets it all sink in. I just hope it will work; I just hope I don't have to have another face-off with Dad. But that's the chance I know I have to take.

Morning is here and no one has come to wake me up. Once I had finally fallen asleep, I slept through the entire night. I wonder if they even read the letter; I wonder why neither of them has come in to get me. I look at the clock, and it's 7:34. Dad will be leaving for work soon. Is he mad? Does he consider what he's read to be false? Did he even bother to read it before he went to bed? I'm not sure what to think. Should I approach him? Should I approach Mom? What does Mom even think? The suspense is starting to irk me as I'm climbing out of bed.

But now I hear it—footsteps approaching from down the hall.

They're heavy, not at all light like Mom's…and they've come to a stop. They've stopped right outside my door. I can no longer hear them, but I know that he is there. I feel him. I can feel him standing right there. He's silent. He's thinking. It is definitely Dad.

He knocks.

My voice creaks, but it tells him to come in.

He does. And he's holding it in his hand—he's holding the letter I had left on his bed.

My eyes have grown large. They watched him as he made his way in; they watched the letter flapping as he held it in his hand. He sits on my bed and pats the spot next to him for me to come join him.

My ears focus in, and my eyes continue to watch him. They spy on his mouth now as it forms a hint of a grin creeping up over his face.

Strangely, this grin is not mean. It's actually a bit sad. I don't know what to think, and really, I have no clue what to say. So I just sit down next to him and I wait.

"Jessica," he begins, "I know that I, well, that we haven't been on the best speaking terms for some time now."

He stops. He stops just as quickly as he had begun. It is quiet. Is he waiting for me to say something? I can't. My mouth won't move. Then he goes on.

"There's something that I should tell you…I just wish that I had figured this all out before."

He stops again. This time, I know he's not waiting for me to talk; he's just trying to figure out how to talk to me. I wait some more. He begins yet again.

"Jessica, I'm really sorry about what's been going on. I'm sorry that I didn't listen to what you were trying to say."

I look into his eyes—they're moist. But still, I can't speak. "This paper, Jessica…This paper is something that your Grandpa should have had." He places it on my lap.

"I know." The words have left my lips. I do know about this thing, this Misophonia. I share it with Grandpa, at least I would if he was still alive.

"Gramma told me, Dad."

"Gramma?" Dad's tear has released. "Your Gramma." His lips form a smile, a smile that is true. But it's not his…it's not Gram ma's…it's one that I have only a memory of, one that used to sneak out from underneath a thick, heavy mustache. It's Grandpa's smile. A smile that I miss, a smile that could have comforted me. One that would have said, "I understand, Jessica. I do. I understand." And I could have answered, "And I understand you too." Grandpa never had that comfort. He never had it, but now I do. And through Grandpa, now Dad can understand me too…I hope so.

I see Dad's mind traveling back in time, filling him with memories; the memories of what was. The memory of what is now—now, with me. Though both of Dad's parents are gone, they have brought him back to me and me to him. I feel my words as they begin to form; I feel them form and I know now that they are true…

"I love you, Dad."

"Oh Jessica, I love you, too."

June

I have completed the 10th grade. It's hard to believe, but I really have. I survived. I did it! I made it to the end. I may not have entered an actual school building, but I've met the requirements. I even passed the MCAS, a test I endured only with great torture. And I'm glad to say that I don't have to see Ms. Mackie anymore! No more of her sniffling…no more of that sound. Ugh, thank God for that! Hopefully I'll have a different tutor when school starts again. Regular high school? No, I won't be doing that. There are just too many sounds—too many sounds that I know I can't handle. Not yet. But maybe someday, and hopefully someday soon. But for now, I will do what I have to do. I will survive this. I will find a way. I will make it through.

Not only that, but there's more. There's another accomplishment that I have recently made. And really, I don't care if I'm the only person who knows or that considers it an accomplishment. For to me, at least, it is a huge accomplishment, one that is important to me. And it is this: I've written and sent out a letter to Abby. We're no longer 'friends' on Facebook, and I have no desire to talk to her by phone. But I wrote her a letter by hand and stuck it in the mail. It didn't travel alone, however. I sent with it the same letter I had shared with Mom and Dad: the letter from the Misophonia website. Now she'll know what it is I have, even though I hadn't wanted to share it with her ever. But now, now I do. It's not so that we can be friends again, but to give our friendship its final and official end. I have grown. I have changed. Abby and I are no longer the same; I could never fit back into her world. And really, I wouldn't ever want to. She is cold. But me, I have become bright, awake. This Misophonia has opened my eyes, and I can see Abby for what she is. And what about me? Lisa was right:

I'm not the anger that tries to hide inside my head. I am me, and nothing else.

Now I sit reading the letter that Abby has mailed back to me. She says that it does sound strange, that my life must really be hard, that I'm right even though she could never understand. She says she is "truly sorry" for our broken relationship. She asks me why I won't reconsider our friendship. But I will never change my mind—I've closed that book. Abby and I are done.

It's strange not missing her. She was always my 'best friend'. It's even more strange, though, that it's actually starting to feel good to be free. I am finally moving on with my life. I am becoming my own. I know who I can trust. I know who is real, and I know what it means to be a real friend: it means sticking in there, not leaving even when things get rough. It's fighting to help even when the resistance

gets tough. I've found a friend like that: Brandon. He kept me alive. He stuck by me and he fought for me when I wanted to die. He waited for me to come back and wouldn't let me go when I did. I don't know if we'll be together forever, but what I do know is that our friendship will always hold. I love him. I love Brandon. He is the one friend that I do know will always be there for me, for what we have is real. He is my one true friend, and he will always be right here.

And so I don't write Abby back. I don't even want to keep her letter—it's already crinkling up and finding the trash bin. As I release it from my hand a smile hikes up my cheeks. The smile of freedom.

The smile of strength. The smile that comes with stress that's finally been released. And so, I can now say it ,and this time for real,...Goodbye, Abby. Goodbye.

It is final. It is my accomplishment. And it is

real.

July

Mom, Dad, and Jeffery are leaving for the parade. They don't bother asking if I want to come; they're already driving away. Jeffery is turning around, smiling at me from the back seat. I see his wide, open-mouthed grin, and his hand waving around like an out-of-control fan. I laugh. I wave and smile back. And yes, I am glad he is gone. He will always be annoying; he'll always make those sounds. But even so, I won't mind seeing him come back, for he is my little brother, and so I love him anyway.

But for now, they're gone and far out of sight. And with them gone, I have time to make something right. To fill in the unsaid. To put my plan into place, a plan that I need to accomplish on my own. Well, maybe with a little help: Brandon and Sharron have come to get me, they will bring me where I need to go.

They drive me away. Each of us quiet, lost in our thoughts, but that's ok. We're comfortable like this. And anyway, our ride is anything but quiet. Our windows are all open, all the way down, with Sharron's CD playing loudly. I'm in the middle seat, sinking into Brandon's arms. I feel the beat of the music thumping into my heart, but I don't care. It's his heartbeat that mine shares; I feel it thumping underneath his shirt, pressing into my ear. The thumping beat persuades my heart to beat in rhythm with his. It's a sound I long to hear. I want it to repeat inside my head, over and over. I'll let it flow, thumping through my ears and beating up into my brain. Thumping, beating, continuing. A sound so good—a sound I so strangely love. How is it that I love that beat? I smile. I really don't know.

We're here.

SOUND

We're all climbing out of the car together, but I walk on alone, down a small grassy hill. The hill is lined with gravestones: tall stones, little stones. Stones that are carved. Stones that are engraved with names.

Names. I see the names. I search through all of the names until I find it—Gramma and Grandpa's gravestones. They're here underneath my feet, underneath my knees. I'm kneeling above their heads, above their bodies that have been deprived of life. Do their spirits linger above my head? Do they see that I am here? I feel the warm breeze whisper through the air; it whispers down, deep inside of me and through me. I feel Gramma and Grandpa here.

"Gramma?" My voice joins the breeze. "Gramma." I want her to hear. I want her to see me. I wish I could see her here. "I found it, Gramma. I know what it is."

I don't know where to focus my eyes, down to the ground or up into the flowing breeze. My fingers feel deep into the crevices of the name carved on Gramma's tombstone. They follow each letter, tracing the letters of her name, and then Grandpa's. I am here now with them. I'm letting them know…

"Gramma, I'm alright. Let Grandpa know that I am ok. Everything has changed." My tears are seeping into the ground over their bodies, over their heads. I wonder if they can feel my tears. I imagine that their cheeks are wet, with my tears and with theirs. The warm breeze blows through my hair, telling me that they are not there— their spirits could never live under that ground—they are here. Right here, and they're listening to me.

"It's ok now. You don't have to watch over me. You can go on up to Heaven. You can be free. I promise you, Gramma, I promise you what I couldn't say before…I will never hurt myself again, Gramma.

I promise. I won't see you until I'm old…but I love you Gramma and Grandpa. I love you so much…"

My head has gone down. My face has

collapsed inside my hands. I feel the warmth of Brandon's hands pressing into my back. He's kneeling down beside me, lifting my eyes to his face. There's a soft smile filling his lips. My body allows him to scoop me up. I'm in his arms. I am crying, and so is he.

A Sneak Preview

how we survive ourselves

by Shaylynn Hayes

Ruth

I'm one on one with my therapist. Each patient is assigned his or her very own mirror. It's not the therapist's job to fix you. That's your job. I wonder what in the hell my parents are actually paying for.

"How are you feeling today, Ruth?" she asks, her voice is calm and soft. Her hair is black and shoulder length. Her face is friendly. She sounds like she cares. Wherever she went to school, they seemingly taught her well. The illusion is convincing.

"The same as the last time," I say.

"There's nothing you want to talk about?" she asks.

This woman is desperate to help me. It must be infuriating when you want to play god but your toys aren't cooperating. If I enjoyed helping people, I'd be annoyed too. I bet she wants to jab me with her pencil. I'm not sure why she doesn't use a pen to write—it's kind of childish to be scribbling notes in a 2HB.

"Nope. I feel the same as before," I say. I want to get this meeting over with so that I can go back to my quiet, white room—pale and plain, with nothing to distract me from the emptiness I'm content to wallow in.

"How did you feel *last* time? Do you want to elaborate?" she asks, all the while that stupid pencil is waiting to take notes on my mental state.

"Nope," I say, not even trying to hide the boredom in my voice.

She taps her pencil on her legal pad.

"This is a safe spot," she says.

"I know," I say. I do know that. That's what people pay for, right? The ability to spill all their deep, dark insecurities on a perfect stranger, all the while going home and re-applying mascara like you aren't some kind of psychopath.

She ends the session. I feel a slight ounce of pity as I walk from her office to my room. It's only four, so we're still allowed to roam freely through the halls. It's not like our doors are locked. The doors that get locked are for people who are a danger to themselves—or to others.

Instead of going directly to my room, I make a turn for the cafeteria. I go because I must eat. I may not want to live, but I'm not suicidal. There's no point in that. They'll stop me. In order to die, you need to have the will to end something. I'm trapped in limbo.

They're serving Caesar salad.

Nona, another one of the doctors, is arguing with a cafeteria worker. She thinks the food should be healthier. Apparently, the pizza they have served the last few nights isn't good enough. I hear her mention that we need better food. Caesar salad has little nutrition. It's a lost cause. The food servers don't care. They make minimum wage.

The doctors are rarely visible except for appointments and rounds. Sometimes they're not even the ones who hold group session. I don't mind. Why should I care about what the doctors do? I don't even care what I do.

I eat my salad bite for bite. There are very few people who remember the old me here.

My mother thinks I'm here because I can't bear the thought of living without my sister. Her problem is that she can't tolerate having two messed up daughters. This is my second time as a live-in mental health patient. The first time never cured me, and I can't imagine the second will either. I guess I do eat more now, so maybe they did do something right.

"Hey," I hear.

It's a boy. He's sitting across the table from me. His name is Lewis, and I'm pretty sure he's here because he was caught selling drugs.

"Hey," I say, and I try not to look at him too closely.

"I didn't see you at group yesterday," he says.

"I was sick," I lie.

"You weren't there last week either."

"Really sick," I lie again.

"Are you coming tomorrow?" he asks.

I think it over. Do I really want to go listen to some teenagers and young adults whine about how we don't get the right cable stations? Do I want to hear the odd rambling about the unfairness of addiction?

"Maybe," I say. It's not like I have anything better to do.

He grins at me. His teeth are showing. They're perfect and white. I wonder if he had braces when he was younger.

"So, I'll see you there?" he asks.

"We'll see," I say. I'm not sure why he cares if I'm there or not. He's probably just bored and trying to fill the time in his court-appointed prison.

Adra

I don't belong with these people. I'm sure their problems are perfectly legitimate, but mine cannot be helped by psychoanalysis. Group sessions are exactly what cause my frustration. People are my frustration. How then, if I cannot stand people, am I supposed to heal in their presence? The answer is that I can't. It's not like I don't want to be helped. I would trade everything I have to end my suffering and finally live a normal life. But I can't.

As I sit here, I'm fighting for my life to be normal. No drugs, no concoctions of science can help me. I'm an outlier. A difference to the rule. The look on other patient's faces says everything I need to know. I am not one of them. My appointments are not filled with goals for recovery—they are met with confusion. Not only mine. I know my doctor doesn't have the answers. He has said so.

Jason sits across from me. He tries his best to seem relatable. Smile on his face, and a man with his heart in the right place. That doesn't matter. He doesn't know how to fix me. I know every patient thinks that—but they are simply ignoring the advice given. Jason truly doesn't understand.

"So, you're anxious about our next group session?" he asks calmly.

I think about nodding but I want to explain. I want him to understand that it's more than anxiety. I settle on, "Yes and no."

"Could you explain what you mean by that?"

"I'm not anxious or worried. I know what's going to happen. I'm dreading it. I know that people will do things that upset me. I know they're going to hurt me."

He presses his hands down on the table. I think it means he's unsure of the situation. "Adra, no one here is trying to hurt you. You know that, right?"

"I'm not demented. I know they're not trying to hurt me. That doesn't change that their sounds bother me. I can't stand the sounds—or the movements—it's like I'm on fire."

He taps his finger on the desk. The match is lit. I want to cry.

"Could you please STOP that?" I snap.

"Stop what?"

How could he know what he's done? No one understands. The movement was enough to raise my internal threat level—I am trapped in a box. He taps his fingers again, this time drilling them.

"Stop tapping your fingers!" I'm closer to a yell. I don't want to explain or rationalize. I want the sounds to stop. I want it to stop now. That's all I can think about as my muscles tense. My heart raises and my chest pounds. "Please stop," I plead. My eyes well with tears.

"Adra, I'm sorry. I don't want to hurt you. I just don't understand why this is so overwhelming to you," he says.

Tears begin falling faster. The fight-flight is running its course, and I feel my muscles almost spasm. "I don't understand either," I say through tears. My voice scuffles.

He no longer moves his fingers and says, "We're going to figure this out. I promise."

How am I supposed to calm down? The movement and noise repeats in my head over and over. I think about how it will happen again. I scrape my fingers across my leg.

"I know... I know... but please promise never to tap your fingers near me. Please," I ask. I've resorted to begging. It keeps playing over and over in my head.

I try to refocus. I try to look at his blue, denim shirt underneath his white coat. I look at his eyes. They are soft and warm, but the event still plays out. I want to cry.

"It's just about time for our group session. Are you going to be okay?" he asks, and he folds his arms to his chest, careful to hide his fingers.

"I..." I know I won't be okay. I'll have to sit in the group meetings. Movements and sounds may be prominent. I close my eyes momentarily, trying to forget the tapping fingers of Claire—or Ruth's irritating sing-song voice.

"Just try. Okay? If it gets too bad, you can just leave early. It'll be okay. I promise."

I nod. Not because I think it will be okay. I nod because Jason is trying his best, and there's no way for me to say no. I don't want him to think I'm not trying. I want him to figure out what's wrong with me.

It's not just sounds—it's movements too. Shaking, tapping, swaying. Anything repetitive sends my brain into a full meltdown.

Caitlin

The kitchen table is filled with sprawled out envelopes. My sister, Jessie, scrunches her nose as she pushes them away from her. She's just seated herself across from me and pushes her Calvin Klein sunglasses to the top of her head.

"Why are you avoiding your bills?" Jessie asks, her nose scrunches more, her eyes, now bare from shades, peer at me.

What she doesn't know is that the bills are spread out to hide one envelope that's different. It's not a bill at all. Instead, it's an emotional hand-grenade.

"I'm not," I say, and I try to back my voice up by straightening my spine.

The re-routed air flow isn't enough to stop her.

"Do you need money?" she asks.

I wish this were about money. I shake my head. She doesn't seem convinced. I must decide whether to pretend I have money issues or explain what's going through my head. I can't figure out which is worse.

"I don't need money," I say. If I said I needed money, she'd cut a check, then continue to ask why I'm not opening the envelopes. She's not going to relent.

Her green eyes feel like daggers as they stare me down. I try to focus on her brown hair. I focus on anything but. Her nose looks sharper when she stares. I contemplate telling her. She'd be so aghast, she'd shut up.

"Then what do you need? What's wrong?" she asks.

I can't tell if she's concerned or nosy. Either or, I push the bills off the envelope and hand it to her. It's unopened. It doesn't have to be opened for me to know the contents. The paper weighs 9,000lbs as far as I'm concerned. I fling it like it's on fire.

Jessie, less concerned about how volatile the contents are, reads the address. She withdraws a deep breath and nods. Instead of opening the envelope, she places it back on the table. I'm both relieved and annoyed. I want the contents to go away, but if it must be dealt with, then she can.

"When's the last time you heard from Riann?" she asks me.

His name hurts to hear out loud.

"I don't know. I send the payments. I don't ask questions. He took off two years ago on a whim. Then after he came back, we agreed he needed help," I say, then I pause for a moment to think. Jessie knows all of this. She doesn't complain as I continue speaking. "I don't know what this is," but I have an idea. I place my hands flat on the table, thinking about my spine again. I make sure it stays straight, and I remain still.

I can see her nose twitching slightly as she says, "You can't avoid this forever."

"Couldn't I? Riann left me first," I say, trying my best to sound confident but failing miserably. As though it changes what I've done. As though his problems are somehow more than my choices.

"Someone left you. But I don't think it was Riann." Jessie says.

"Whomever left still left. And now he's there," I say.

"He's not on vacation, he's in a mental health facility," Jessie says. Compared to living out in the real world, I wonder if it is a vacation.

I notice one of the buttons on my white blouse is undone, and I fiddle with it before pushing the button back through the tiny hole. I make a game of taking as long as possible.

"Caitlin," she says my name with a sigh. "Listen to me. You have to tell him."

"And if I tell him and then lose him again?"

"Cheap cop out," Jessie says, and she rolls her eyes at me. "Lose him? You've only talked to him through phone calls for two years. You've already lost him."

"You know what I mean. How can I know what will happen if I hurt him like this?"

I watch her eyes turn to Garret who's sitting in the highchair playing with blocks. He has my light blond hair instead of his father's darker shade but the unmistakable eyes of his father.

"If you're not going to do it for Riann, at least tell him for Garrett," she says, and she pushes the envelope back to me. "Open it."

She has me cornered. No matter what I say, it's going to relay back to her words 'open it'.

I watch Garrett, who looks so peaceful as he smashes a red and blue block together—not even caring that they're on the wrong side to connect. My hands shake as I tear at the cream paper.

I skim the contents. I let my eyes fall only on the most important words. Jessie's eyes never move from me. I fold the paper on the crease, but she reaches out her hands before I can put it back in the envelope.

It's easier to give in. I hand her the paper, and she reads. I can no longer sit. My entire body feels like a wave pool. I reach out for Garrett, and he puts his arms up for me to carry him. I wrap my arms around him and carry him around the kitchen. Dirty dishes are piled on the counter, and the sink itself has soap scuds. I'm a terrible housewife for more than one reason.

"He wants to see you," Jessie finally says aloud.

"Yes," I say as I nod. "He does."

I keep pacing so that I don't feel her eyes on me.

"Are you going to go?" she asks.

"I think I have to."

Misophonia Resources

Want to read more books about Misophonia? Check out:

How We Survive Ourselves(Fiction), Full of Sound and Fury (Non-Fiction) and Exploring Misophonia (Non Fiction).

For more misophonia resources go to www.misophoniaeducation.com and www.misophoniainternational.com

Made in the USA
Las Vegas, NV
15 June 2021

24810389R00166